They went on kissing and kissing and kissing

without restraint, with more and more zeal, more vigorous tongue-play, deepening that kiss and raising an ever greater appetite in her until Marli lost all track of time, of everything but kissing him.

But just about the time she began to recognize that, for the second night in a row, Dalton seemed to have more wherewithal than she did and gradually reversed things, pulling out of that kiss to drop his forehead to her hairline with a sigh. "I wasn't going to do that again..." he said in a whisper.

"Me neither," she whispered back.

But they stayed the way they were, head-to-head, both of her hands on his chest now, his hand behind her head and his arm around her also keeping them together.

They sat there that way for too long for it not to be clear that there was no eagerness to separate.

Dear Reader,

We're back in the small town of Merritt, Montana, where Dalton—the fourth Camden brother—has been ordered to decide whether or not to court-martial his childhood nemesis, Holt Abbott. What Dalton hadn't expected to find there was Marli Abbott, Holt's sister and Dalton's onetime love.

Marli, whose goal was to get out and stay out of the small town, has recently changed her mind and decided to move back. Knowing that Dalton was a career marine—like her brother until he was injured in the line of duty—she hadn't expected to see the person who had meant more to her than anyone. The person she'd had to hurt.

Dalton hasn't forgotten—or forgiven—how she left him. And now he holds her brother's fate in his hands. It's finally time for her to explain, to make amends and maybe to help herself get over the past, if it's possible.

I hope you enjoy reading this as much as I enjoyed writing it.

Best,

Victoria Pade

The Marine's Second Chance

VICTORIA PADE

HARLEQUIN

SPECIAL
EDITION

Recycling programs
for this product may
not exist in your area.

ISBN-13: 978-1-335-72462-5

The Marine's Second Chance

Harlequin Enterprises ULC
22 Adelaide St. West, 41st Floor
Toronto, Ontario M5H 4E3, Canada
www.Harlequin.com

Printed in U.S.A.

Victoria Pade is a *USA TODAY* bestselling author of numerous romance novels. She has two beautiful and talented daughters—Cori and Erin—and is a native of Colorado, where she lives and writes. A devoted chocolate lover, she's in search of the perfect chocolate chip cookie recipe.

For information about her latest and upcoming releases, visit Victoria on Facebook—she would love to hear from you.

Chapter One

It was a bad day for Marli Abbott to be running late. But the rental agent had called on that June Saturday morning and said if she didn't sign the lease on her new office immediately, the other interested party was going to swoop it out from under her. So she'd had to rush from the family farm where she'd grown up just outside of Merritt, Montana, and go into the heart of her small hometown to sign the lease.

After getting that done as fast as she could, she hurried back home at a breakneck speed, hoping the quiet country roads weren't being patrolled by any traffic officer with a speeding ticket quota to fill. Luckily they weren't, and she turned from the main road onto the driveway with a full twenty minutes to get herself ready to take the rest of that Saturday off.

The driveway ran alongside the two-story farmhouse and took her all the way back to the garage behind the house, where she parked her black sedan. Then she got out and hurried to the small guest cottage for a shower.

When she'd decided to move back to Merritt, it had been her intention to live in the main house. She and her older brother had inherited the house and guest cottage, plus fifty acres of farmland, which they leased to a neighbor, from their mother two years earlier. As a career marine, Holt had had no intention of living anywhere on the property himself. But then fate had altered her brother's future and the house had turned out to be where he and his wife, Bridget, needed to go. So Marli had taken the cottage.

She threw off the clothes she'd thrown on, released her long auburn hair from its slapdash ponytail and got into the shower, already thinking ahead to what the rest of the day held. It would mostly consist of being there for Holt and Bridget as they worked through another milestone in her brother's new situation.

Since his release from a veterans' rehabilitation center two days ago, Marli and Bridget had been combining their energies and ideas to help settle him in at home. Some modifications were temporary, only needed until he got more of his strength and health back. Others required a more permanent shift. Holt now had paraplegia and required a wheelchair to get around. It was a challenging adjustment on multiple levels—not least because the old house was not built with wheelchair accessibility in mind.

Today would mark his first bath here—with help from Louise, the local nurse, and old friend Yancy Coltrain. While Marli didn't intend to be in on the actual bathing, she had promised to be on hand for whatever else might come up.

She showered and dried off quickly, then flipped over and brushed her hair from the underside up to gather it at her crown before twisting it around itself and holding the haphazard knot in place with two hairpins.

She was in too much of a hurry for moisturizer and makeup, so to compensate for the absence, she pinched her high cheekbones to add some color, applied a swipe of lip gloss to her lips and regretted that she would be seeing old acquaintance Yancy for the first time since high school looking like she did. But there just wasn't the opportunity for more, not even for a touch of mascara to highlight her pale green eyes.

She dressed in the first things that came to hand— undies, an ancient bra, a pair of black yoga pants and a white V-neck T-shirt that were all usually left as lounging-around-on-a-lazy-day attire.

Then she slipped her bare feet into a pair of nondescript black ballet flats and out the door she went again.

"I'm back. Did I make it?" she called as she flung open the back door into the main house.

"I'm watching for them but nobody's here yet," Bridget replied from the living room. "Did you hear that, honey?" she added.

"I heard," Marli's brother answered from the dining room they'd converted into a bedroom.

Marli found her tall, blonde Nordic-looking sister-in-law standing at the picture window in the living room and joined her there.

"I'm glad you got here—I was hoping you would, since I've never met this Yancy guy even though Holt says he's one of his best friends." Bridget wasn't from Merritt.

"He's Holt's age but we all grew up together," Marli explained. "He's a nice guy. You'll like him."

"Do you think he's strong enough for the job? Holt says he was always really skinny…"

"Yeah, but he's a farm boy. I think if he can hoist bales of hay, he can help with this."

"I'm relieved that the nurse is coming, too, so she can make sure we get Holt in and out of the tub the best way."

"Her name is Louise, right?" Marli asked just to make sure.

"Right. And the doctor is—"

"Joan—she wasn't here before, either, so I haven't met her yet at all." The nurse had made the initial house call the day before to check that Holt had weathered the trip from Virginia all right, so they *had* met her.

"And the nurse will call the doctor once the bath is finished and the doctor will actually make a house call, too," Bridget concluded. "It's really nice that they're making so much extra effort. I didn't expect that."

"Small town," Marli said by way of explanation.

Two cars pulled into the driveway then.

"They're here," Bridget called to Holt as Marli went outside.

She crossed the front porch, skirted the ramp she and Bridget had installed over the left side of the three steps and used the still-exposed right side of the stairs to go down into the yard.

The nurse got out of the closest car first, exchanged greetings with Marli and then said she wanted a few minutes with Holt before they got started. She went inside just as Yancy slid from behind the steering wheel of his dingy blue-green truck and rounded the front end.

"Hello, Mr. Coltrain," Marli said in mock formality.

"Is that really you, Marli? Long time no see," the tall, thin man responded. "All grown up and...wow!"

"Oh, right." Marli deflected the flattery she wasn't buying in to and lobbed a little back. "Look at you—you haven't aged a day!" Which was true—Yancy still had gaunt, homely boy-next-door features under kinky-curly dirty-blond hair.

"Yeah, I know," he said ruefully. "Who wants to be so baby-faced at thirty-five that they still get asked for ID to order a beer?"

"Everybody around here knows you, so if anyone is asking for your ID, they're just doing it to mess with you," Marli said laughingly as Yancy bent down to give her a big bear hug.

Over his shoulder she caught a glimpse of a newer-model white truck turning into the driveway of the Camden farm across the street. The truck stopped abruptly.

Marli ended the hug with Yancy but her attention didn't instantly return to him. It stayed on the white truck and the fact that it hadn't gone any farther up the drive.

Noticing her distraction, Yancy pivoted slightly to peer in the same direction. "Waitin' for one of the Camdens to throw rocks at you?" the tall man joked.

He was kidding…mostly. Relations between the Abbotts and the Camdens had had some difficulties over the years. Difficulties that had caused a festering grudge in Holt. A grudge he'd held against Dalton Camden in particular from the time they were all children. A grudge that could now put Holt's future in jeopardy.

And certainly Marli knew that her own actions toward Dalton seventeen years ago hadn't made things better…

"No," Marli answered, pretending she wasn't nervous herself about what she might be facing from the

Camden family now that she'd moved back. "In fact, Ben Camden came over to chat this morning while Holt and Bridget and I were having breakfast on the front porch. He said that if there was anything we needed, anything he could do, to just call."

"Yeah, that sounds like old Ben—he's a peace-maker."

Marli had been relieved to discover that was the elder Camden's attitude because she'd had no idea what kind of bad light the family might see her in after the way she'd left Merritt. And Dalton.

The decision seemed to have been made at least by the Camden grandfather to keep things civil— which sounded good to her. But that made it odd that the truck still wasn't moving up the driveway.

"Maybe today Ben wants to say hello to you?" Marli postulated. She'd spotted the elderly man be-hind the wheel just as he'd made the turn.

"Don't know why. I just saw him at the lodge last night," Yancy informed her.

Then the white truck's passenger door opened. Marli hadn't even noticed that there *was* a passen-ger before the man got out.

From the distance and the angle, she could ini-tially tell only that it was a man dressed in a marine utility uniform.

But that was enough to cause her concern.

Marli kept on watching as the man rounded the front of the truck, stopped to say something to Ben and then went to the truck bed to remove a large duffel bag, setting it on the drive.

Please let it be anyone but him...

Anyone but the person who held her brother's fate in his hands.

The person she'd done very, very wrong.

The man began to cross the road but Marli continued to hold on to some denial because—as irrational as it was—this clearly wasn't the not-much-more-than-a-boy she'd last seen.

This was a full-grown man. A tall, broad-shouldered, strapping, imposing man with an air of someone to be reckoned with.

This was certainly not the Dalton she remembered.

Not the Dalton who had been her childhood best friend, who had slowly become more, who had been all of her firsts. Who—once upon a time—she'd cared for...

Loved...

As he drew nearer, she focused on more details, hanging on to any basis for denial.

No, the hair wasn't longish the way Dalton's had been the last time she'd seen him, but this man's short-on-the-sides, slightly longer-on-top hair was that same brown-almost-black color.

And no, as she began to see his face better, it wasn't the face of the merely cute teenage boy she'd known. Instead the baby fat had been chiseled down to reveal a well-sculpted bone structure that formed a straight, thin nose; a sharp jawline; and an all-around starkly handsome, supremely masculine face shadowed in just a hint of dark stubble that the Dalton she'd been familiar with hadn't been capable of.

But it was the blue eyes that finally forced her to shatter her disavowal of who this was. Those bright cobalt-blue eyes that the Camdens were known for. Those bright cobalt-blue eyes she knew all too well.

There was no denying it any longer. This had to be the Dalton of now.

But his slightly bushy brows were stern over those blue eyes, which shot daggers. His sensual not-too-full lips were a harsh, serious line. And there was nothing friendly about this expression, which she had never before seen from him.

In fact, there was so much coldness emanating from him that it actually made a shiver run through Marli. She was left with no doubt that he'd become a very hard man who bore her only ill will.

Which wasn't apt to help her brother any.

"Holt has thirty more days of medical leave," she heard herself blurt out defensively. "You can't take him anywhere."

"I came to make sure he's here and that he stays put. For now," Dalton said in a voice that was deeper than it had been and left no question that he was secure in and comfortable with his authority.

"Your grandfather saw us all early this morning, so he can verify that Holt is here. But he's with a nurse right now, so it would be better if you left him alone. Forever…" she added as wishful thinking.

"I won't be leaving him alone forever," Dalton warned.

"You'll let him *stay put* for now, though," she said, repeating Dalton's own words with a hopeful intonation. "To get these last thirty days of rest and recovery…so he doesn't have to do that locked up…"

"I haven't decided yet. But make no mistake about where this is leaning. For damn good reason."

Marli knew there *was* good reason, so there was nothing to say to that. Instead she maintained a sentry-like stance, raised a defiant chin to conceal how unnerved she actually was and said, "Well, it sounds like nothing is happening today. So since Holt's nurse and Yancy are here to help Holt have a bath, maybe you should just go."

Those Camden blue eyes slowly went to their old acquaintance still standing near Marli, watching the back-and-forth.

"Yancy," Dalton said flatly, more in acknowledgment than salutation.

"Dalton," Yancy answered with clear reservation.

The Camden blue eyes returned to Marli, settling on her as if taking stock and sizing her up.

It made her terribly uncomfortable, but she wasn't about to let it show. She just met him eye to eye in a stare down that went on long enough for Yancy to shuffle his feet and nervously clear his throat.

Then Dalton said, "I'll be back. Marli."

The contempt in the way he said her name was jarring. Concealing that, too, she merely raised her chin another tick. "Dalton," she returned with equal challenge.

Which seemed to have no effect on him as he turned and retraced his steps across the road.

Marli watched him go, struck by the breadth and strength in his back as he did.

When he reached the Camden driveway, he bent to grab his duffel bag in an angry swipe then straightened again to take it with him up the drive.

"S'pose he didn't leave that in the truck because he didn't want old Ben to carry it in while he came over here," Yancy murmured as if thinking aloud.

But the duffel bag was the last thing on Marli's mind.

She was still taken aback by what she'd just seen and heard.

And the knowledge that, like her brother, she'd earned the wrath of Dalton Camden. She likely should have expected that.

But even so, even with seventeen years of nothing between them, it still hurt…

Chapter Two

"Oh, man, Pops, you can't keep feeding me like you have today! It's a good thing you have some hard labor for me to do while I'm here," Dalton said with a groan as he and his three brothers gathered around the big farmhouse kitchen table.

After his arrival this morning, his grandfather had fixed him a big lunch before Dalton had taken a nap to conquer some jet lag from the eighteen-hour trip he'd made from overseas. By the time he woke up, his brothers and all three of their fiancées—along with his brother Tanner's surprise three-month old daughter, Poppy—had all come for the family barbecue.

Dalton's complaint wasn't real, though. It had been great to have Ben's home cooking. And great, too, to be with his grandfather, to have his brothers in one place and to catch up with the women who would become his sisters-in-law—all of them had been raised in Merritt, so not unknown to him, just long unseen. And then there was his new niece—he was still trying to wrap his head around the fact that Tanner had a kid.

The women—Lexie Parker, Addie Markham and Clairy McKinnon—had won the coin toss that determined who was on cleanup duty. They were now relaxing together out back with Poppy. The men had just finished that cleanup and treated themselves to one more round of the beers Micah had brought from his brewery.

"How long since you've been home?" Quinn asked Dalton.

"Too long!" Ben answered before Dalton had the chance. The elder Camden took a chair at the table, too. "None of you could get home as much as I wanted, and I can't tell you how happy I am that you other three are back in Merritt for good now. But this one? Four times in seventeen years! That's all!"

And he'd kept even those visits as short as he could. Dalton felt bad about that. But thanks to Marli Abbott, he'd left town for Annapolis with ugly memories and a bitter taste in his mouth. Every time he'd returned to Merritt he'd just relived it all. It had given him no inclination to stick around to wallow in that misery. Or return for more anytime soon once he'd gotten away again.

"I haven't been good about coming home. I'm sorry, Pops," he apologized rather than attempt to deny the truth. "But we've still seen each other—I bring you to wherever I am when it works out for us both. And we had that month together in Italy the summer before last—that was nice."

"And a trip I'll never forget. But you still don't come home enough."

"Guilty as charged," Dalton conceded.

"Speaking of guilt and charges…" Micah chimed in. "Holt Abbott…what the hell happened?"

"We know you were assigned command of that mission in Syria to bring back the senator's teenage daughter and her two friends," Tanner put in.

"That's right—they were radicalized by ISIS over the internet and lured there, weren't they?" Quinn added.

"They were," Dalton confirmed. "Because Abbott had some experience in the area where the girls were being held, he and four men from his unit were assigned to go along with my team. Under my command—"

"Because you're a major and he's a captain," Micah pointed out.

"And it was my mission, not his."

"The marines haven't learned by now to keep you and Holt Abbott as far apart as they can?" Ben asked.

"That isn't the way the marines operate," Micah said with a laugh. "Although you'd think they'd make an exception since you kept on fighting all through Annapolis and—"

"And every time your paths have crossed since,"

Quinn interjected. "You've always brought out the worst in each other."

Again there was no sense denying the truth, so Dalton didn't try. He merely went on with his answer. "My unit had surveilled the abandoned church where the girls were being held and the surrounding area before Abbott and his men got there. There were too many explosive booby traps all around the place to go in without some light, so I set the mission for dawn. Abbott got there and…well, he did what he's always done when it comes to me—he disagreed."

"Probably didn't help that you'd been promoted ahead of him after years of the two of you being neck and neck rising through the ranks. Having you as his superior officer must have stuck in his craw," Quinn guessed.

"Oh, yeah," Dalton said with disgust.

"And he was belligerent as always—" Tanner said.

"And hoping to show you up so he could be the big hero and land in the senator's good graces," Micah added.

Dalton acknowledged both points with the raise of his chin before he continued. "He said he could spot the booby traps even in the dark and should take the lead. I overrode him and gave the order for the mission to go on as planned. At sunrise—"

"He disobeyed a direct order?" Ben asked. From his own brief stint in the army, he was clearly aware that there weren't many offenses in any branch of the military greater than that.

"He did," Dalton confirmed. "He enlisted the four

men he'd brought with him and led them out at 2:00 a.m. He got about thirty yards inside the perimeter and hit a booby trap. All four of his men were injured to lesser extents, the ISIS rebels were alerted and—"

"What you'd designed as an organized, controlled mission went sideways," Quinn finished for him.

"It turned into a battle and we had to not only rescue the civilians while under fire, but Holt and his men, too."

"Which—to your credit—you did," Tanner concluded.

"With no injuries to the teenagers or your unit," Micah said proudly.

"And Holt and his men?" Ben inquired. "I saw him in the wheelchair when he got here but I haven't heard any specifics about his injuries… I was hoping maybe it was a temporary condition…"

"He suffered a severe spinal injury. He's permanently lost the use of his legs. His men were hurt to varying degrees but have all made full recoveries and are back on duty."

"And now that he's in the last stage of rehab, it's time to face the music," Quinn said.

"Colonel Lundquist is a friend of the Senator's, he assigned me the mission," Dalton went on. "The Senator was glad to have his daughter and her friends brought out safely but not happy about the injuries that made it look as if he was sacrificing service members for his own personal agenda. He also wasn't pleased that his daughter ended up in an active battle. The colonel is plenty pissed off himself and wants Holt brought up on charges—"

"But it was your mission and your orders that Abbott disobeyed," Tanner summarized. "So it's you who has to make the decision about having him court-martialed. Or not."

"And Colonel Lundquist sent me here to make that decision. And to make sure Holt doesn't go AWOL to avoid accountability."

Silence fell over all five men with the weight of the conversation and the situation they were discussing hanging in the air.

Then, soft-hearted Ben asked, "Do you have other options besides a court-martial that would appease the higher-ups?"

All four brothers were marines and knew well what was on the table. It was Quinn who said, "The other options are administrative action—that would be a slap on the wrist. Or nonjudicial punishment, which is for minor misconduct—"

"Or, because it was Dalton's order and this is at his discretion, he can take no action—" Micah added.

"But," Tanner said in a voice of reason, "if he decides on less than the court-martial that the colonel wants, that puts his own ass on the line. For Holt Abbott."

"And with the way things have always been between the two of you—"

Dalton cut off his grandfather. "That's why he disobeyed the orders—because he still has a chip on his shoulder over some damn ancient grudge!" Dalton's own anger at being in this position had risen to the surface but he took a long pull on his beer to get it under control.

"And you know Marli Abbott is here?" Quinn said, treading more carefully into that subject.

"I saw her." Dalton nearly growled the words. "I didn't think she'd be here, of all places."

"She's in the process of moving back…" Micah offered, equally as warily as Quinn had.

"To live? In Merritt? For good?" Dalton responded, shocked.

Micah nodded his head to confirm that.

Dalton had assumed Marli was just in town to look after her brother—that was bad enough. But she'd actually returned to live in their old hometown? The thought of that made Dalton see red. "Are you kidding me? She couldn't wait to leave!" he nearly bellowed. "Her whole goal in life was to get out and stay out!" Even when it meant leaving him in her dust. Completely.

But before more could be said, the back door opened and in came Lexie for a drink refill, halting their conversation.

"If you guys are done with the cleanup, what are you doing still in this hot kitchen when it's so nice outside?"

"She's right," Micah agreed with his fiancée, getting to his feet.

Tanner, Quinn and their grandfather followed suit. "Come on," Quinn said to Dalton on their way out. "Enough about the Abbotts. Let's just enjoy tonight."

"I'll be there in a minute," Dalton assured them.

He needed a moment to himself, to let this news of Marli settle in.

He couldn't believe she'd moved back to Merritt. He hadn't bargained for her being here at all. He'd thought the worst he would have to deal with was her brother.

But there she'd been this morning.

It was the first time he'd set eyes on her since that day he'd driven her home from the clinic in Billings when they were teenagers.

And yet one look at her this morning had shot him into the past and made him shout for his grandfather to stop the truck so he could get out and go over there...

The minute he'd exited the truck, he'd been disgusted with his own actions.

What the hell are you doing? he'd silently berated himself.

After seventeen years, after her tossing him away like an old used-up rag and never looking back, a single glimpse of her had sent him running?

What was wrong with him?

She's nothing to you, he'd told himself even as he'd started across that road. *Not a friend, nothing but a bad memory of how big a sucker you were to think you were ever anything to her but a stupid kid she could lead around by the nose.*

"But those days are over," he said under his breath now. Marli Abbott honestly was nothing to him.

Nothing but a part of his childhood.

Nothing but a harsh eye-opener at the end of his teenage years.

Nothing but another damn Abbott he had history with and now had to contend with.

But when it came to Marli, history was all there was to it. Ancient history, dead and buried. His reaction to seeing her this morning must have just been a lack of sleep and jet lag—plus shock that after so much time and heartache she was right there again…

And maybe his reaction had been out of some kind of weird need to get close enough to make sure his eyes weren't deceiving him. Because after all, she didn't look exactly the way she had way back when.

Way back when, when she'd been somewhere between a girl and a woman…

A pretty girl but not the head turner who had caught his attention this morning.

Now the brown hair that had once only reached her chin had become a thick mane of shiny auburn. He wasn't sure of the length, but it had to be much longer to make that full knot she'd had at the crown of her head.

Now her uneven teenage skin had turned flawlessly clear and as smooth and pristine as alabaster.

Now her perky nose was slender and straight. Her lips were lush, her bone structure not only delicate but refined.

And those unusual pale green eyes she'd had as a kid? They'd darkened slightly but become luminous and streaked with silver—making them even more unusual. More unique. More beautiful…

Plus she'd filled out into some curves that would have driven him even wilder than her pre-woman's body had...

But whether she was all-around breathtaking or not didn't make any difference to him. He'd endured the hell she'd put him through and finally gotten over her to move on with his life. The same way she'd moved on with hers.

"She's just going to be an extra pain in the ass," he complained as if he were talking to someone else, focusing on his aggravation rather than on any hint of curiosity or attraction or interest in her.

After today's interaction with her, it was clear that she was an obstacle willing to get between him and Holt, making the situation that much messier and more complicated.

But he was Holt's ranking officer and he wouldn't let her get in the way of doing his duty.

He did realize, though, that he was going to have to guard himself against being influenced by the way they'd parted. Whatever he decided to do with Holt, it couldn't be payback to Marli.

Regardless of how tempting it might be to strike back at two birds with one stone...

It was just a damn good thing for both of them that the marine in him was well disciplined enough to keep himself and his actions in control.

Something neither of the Abbotts could lay claim to.

"He's asleep already," Bridget announced quietly as she joined Marli in the kitchen.

It wasn't even eight o'clock yet and Marli was just finishing loading their dinner dishes into the dishwasher.

"He had a full day. And right after a travel day that he didn't get to rest up from," Marli said.

"We got it all done, though—the bath, the doctor's visit, the physical, even his haircut. He said he finally felt human again with the buzz cut. I kind of liked it longish, though."

"The buzz cut makes him look more intense—I think that's what he likes about it. You know, he likes the tough-guy thing. He always has."

"Holt calls the buzz cut the marine cut, but when the major was here I noticed he doesn't wear his hair like that…"

Marli closed the dishwasher and turned to lean against the sink to face her sister-in-law. It sounded so strange to hear Bridget call Dalton *the major*. And to also hear the fearful deference in Bridget's voice that told Marli just how afraid Bridget was of Dalton and what he could do to Holt.

He wasn't *the major* to Marli.

But what was he?

In her mind over the years—until seeing him again this morning—he'd been just Dalton. Her childhood best friend, her partner in mischief and then her partner in much more. He was someone who—in the end—she'd treated badly. Someone who hadn't deserved what she'd done in fleeing Merritt—something that had produced the intense shame she'd felt every time she'd thought about him since then.

But now he was something else, too. He was some-one who had power and authority over Holt. Some-one who had presented an unsettling appearance of strength and hostility today.

"This was the first time I've ever seen him," Bridget was saying. "Holt has talked about him before—Holt calls him his archenemy. Actually that's the nicest thing he calls him… I know they're the same age, but after listening to Holt talk about him, I pictured him as one of those old bulldog-faced, mean-looking, never-smile marines. From what I saw through the living room window this morning, he's mean looking and unsmiling, but the face is anything but bulldog. He's some kind of hot…"

Every kind, actually, Marli thought, almost as as-tonished as her friend was at the way Dalton looked now. It was a mental picture she'd found impossible to get out of her head today, despite how busy she'd been. Or how hard she'd tried. And she'd tried re-ally, really hard.

But Bridget was right—Dalton had had a mean expression on that handsome face and he'd been a very, very long way from smiling.

"Is that how he's always been?" her friend asked. "Hot but scary-mean?"

"He wasn't really hot growing up. Nice-looking, cute… He definitely improved with age…" Remark-ably in fact. "And he didn't used to be scary-mean, either—that's not a side of him I've ever seen before. When he and Holt would get into it growing up, Dalton never backed down and he was a fierce foe. But the way he was today? That's not the Dalton *I* knew."

But talking about him wasn't helping her to stop thinking about him, so Marli changed the subject. "If there's nothing else you need me for over here, I think I'll head back to the cottage to do some unpacking."

Bridget nodded, but before Marli could move from the sink, Bridget said, "I don't think I've thanked you for letting us have the house. I know you planned on living in it yourself and now you're stuck out in the cottage."

No, that hadn't been the plan. But then returning to Merritt hadn't ever been part of her plan, either. Plans changed.

Seventeen years ago, a panicked seventeen-year-old Marli had believed that if she didn't escape Merritt and her feelings for Dalton, she would end up cemented in the small town, living the same life in the same place that her mother had blamed for her own desperate unhappiness.

So when, just days after Holt's high school graduation, the opportunity to get away had presented itself, Marli had seen it as destiny opening a door for her and she'd wormed her way through it.

Once she and her mother, Ginger, were in Los Angeles with Ginger's ailing sister, Marli had begged to stay, hoping never—ever—to go back.

With Holt headed for the naval academy at the end of that summer, Ginger had seen an opportunity of her own to finally get out of the small town she hated, to start over herself, and she'd jumped on her young daughter's bandwagon.

She'd kept the property in Merritt, though, leasing the fields that went with the farmhouse and renting out the house itself. The money she'd made had been her primary income, covering the cost of moving to California and setting up a new life for herself there.

When Ginger died suddenly two years ago, Holt and Marli had inherited everything equally. They'd decided to continue leasing the land and renting the house. But eleven months ago Marli's own life had hit a major bump that had caused her to reevaluate what she wanted from life. And although it shocked her, she'd suddenly found appeal in returning to Merritt.

Since Holt had every intention of being a career marine, he'd had no need for the house and had been agreeable to her moving in.

But just as Marli had sold her portion of a Denver acupuncture practice, Holt had been injured. Rather than moving directly from Denver to Merritt as planned, Marli had sent her belongings into storage and headed straight to her brother's side. For the last eight months she and Bridget had been scraping by, sharing dingy motel rooms and dingier month-to-month furnished apartments as close as they could get to Holt's various treatment centers, following him from one surgery to another, from one recovery center to another, to oversee his care and make sure he was getting the best the military had to offer.

Once it had become obvious that Holt's future as

a marine was at an end, he and Bridget had realized they needed the house. So it had only made sense for Marli to give it over to them.

"I don't mind the cottage," she assured. "We gave the last renters permission to completely remodel it for the wife's mother to live in and it's really nice. Besides, it wouldn't make sense for me to have the whole house to myself. It's better suited to a family— you and Holt and those kids you keep talking about having. Plus there's Holt's chair—the cottage might be one floor but with all the tight corners, it would be even worse for that."

"Still…" Bridget said, "I feel like we took the house out from under you."

"It's no big deal, Bridge. Really," Marli answered honestly. Bridget and Holt had had a whirlwind romance after they'd met when Bridget was a translator in Okinawa, where Holt had been stationed. Marli hadn't even had a chance to meet her before she and Holt eloped. But Marli had spent so much time with Bridget during the last eight months that they'd become close friends. "I'm happy to have less space to take care of while I get my office opened and my business started again here."

"And you already found an office when you came last week to get your stuff out of storage?"

"I did. It's perfect—needs a little paint but it's right in the center of town, right on Independence. I told the agent I didn't even need to see any other spaces— not that there are many available. I've got a one-year lease—long enough to see if I can drum up enough business for the expense of a separate office space to make sense. If not, I might end up putting an office in the garage. We'll see."

"Turning the garage into an office would be okay, too, though. It could help make up for us taking the house—"

Bridget's words were cut off by a knock on the front door loud enough to startle them both.

"Whoa! Who's that?" Marli asked.

The front door was oak with an oval of beveled glass mere inches from both the top and bottom of the door that made much of who and what was beyond it visible. Just a few steps out of the kitchen, Marli could see Dalton standing on the porch.

His back was to the door, his hands clasped military fashion over a rear end that had also improved with time. A lot.

Annoyed with herself for recognizing that, she raised her gaze, but her appreciation wasn't lessened by the sight of his powerful-looking back and shoulders.

In fact, something inside her fluttered. She firmly told herself it was tension, not a response to him.

Then he turned to face the door for another pounding knock and the flutter hit harder at her second glimpse of just what a jaw-droppingly handsome man he'd grown into.

A very *angry* handsome man, because the expression on that starkly chiseled face was fierce, drawing his slightly bushy eyebrows closer to the two vertical lines between them that said *I dare you to mess with me*...

Keeping her voice low enough not to be heard outside, she informed Bridget, who was trailing her, "It's Dalton again…"

"Oh, God…" Bridget whispered.

"It's okay. Don't worry. Go upstairs. I'll handle it," Marli assured her quietly.

Bridget fled up the stairs behind Marli as Marli opened the door.

Before she could even greet Dalton, he said, "I need to see your brother."

"Hello to you, too," she answered, her tone snide.

The screen door had been removed to make it easier for Holt to get through, so they were standing there without anything between them, on an equal platform. It made Marli realize that she was looking up higher at Dalton than she had seventeen years ago. She judged that he was about three inches taller than the six feet he'd been when they'd parted at seventeen and eighteen—something she hadn't noticed in the yard this morning.

He'd also changed clothes—he was wearing camo pants and a plain white crew neck T-shirt. But unlike the looser shirt of the utility uniform he'd had on earlier, the T-shirt snugly hugged—and highlighted—impressive muscles, both in his expansive chest and in biceps that stretched the sleeves to their limit.

Despite the more casual attire, he still had an air of authority, though. And that attitude, that increase in height, those muscles and even the dark,

dark shadow of stubble on his face that seemed to shout of his boost in masculinity made Marli feel at a disadvantage. A disadvantage that struck a sour note in her.

"I need to see your brother," he repeated sternly, disregarding her sarcastic greeting.

"Today exhausted him and Holt is already asleep," she informed succinctly.

"I took your word and my grandfather's for it earlier but now I have to put eyes on him so I know he's really here. I don't care if he's awake or asleep."

There was so much animosity in Dalton's deep voice. Even when they'd argued growing up, he'd never spoken to her like that. Only this morning had she heard it before.

She wasn't sure why, but it just made her bristle even more. "You might be the boss of everybody else, but you're not the boss of me," she said bluntly. "Go home and come back tomorrow."

"One phone call is all it would take for me to have your brother carted out of here and put under lock and key in a brig hospital ward for the next thirty days. Just because I didn't set that into motion earlier today doesn't mean I can't still do it. Or that I won't," he threatened.

"I wouldn't let you do it without a fight, and you know I can mount a good one if I put my mind to it."

That made one corner of Dalton's perfectly shaped mouth twitch. In another man, it might have looked like the start of a smile. But this time there was something different to it, something that seemed smug. "I might enjoy watching that," he said. "But it wouldn't do you any good."

The coldness and contempt in his voice sent a chill through her. More so because it was coming from Dalton. Dalton, who had always been her greatest defender. That coldness and contempt made it sound as if he hated her.

It wasn't easy to adjust her thinking to that.

But she reminded herself that she'd left him behind without a word. That she'd followed that up by not answering so much as a single call, a single message, a single email from him—no matter how frantically he'd pleaded with her to let him know she was all right. She hadn't even given him a reprieve when Holt had gloated about how he was tormenting Dalton the entire rest of that summer every time Dalton tried to persuade Holt to tell him how she was, where she was, to relay a message to her, to have her call him.

It was a terrible thing to have done to him. It didn't matter that she had also paid dearly for it herself. Now she was witnessing how it had not only cost her Dalton, but her right to his loyalty, to his friendship, to any scrap of concern from him or any kind of consideration for her.

It was something she realized she'd better keep in mind now as well-earned guilt took her indignation down a peg. And she also reminded herself that when it came to her brother, Dalton *did* have the advantage. If she didn't take that seriously enough, she could make things worse.

So she said, "You can poke your head into his room if you promise not to disturb him. Remember that his doctors prescribed one last month of rest and recuperation before getting on with things."

"I don't need to *disturb* him. I need to see that he's here and hasn't used this move to go AWOL. I shouldn't have even given him today."

"You're overestimating his strength at this point," Marli said even as she moved out of the doorway so Dalton could come inside.

He stepped in without waiting for more invitation and glanced up the stairs.

"Is he in his old room?" Dalton asked.

"No, we can't get him up there yet—maybe ever. We're still figuring out all the changes that have to be made to the house."

"Take me to wherever he is," Dalton said as if nothing else mattered to him.

Marli knew the two men hadn't seen each other since the explosion and wondered if Dalton had any idea what her brother was dealing with now. As she led the way back to the kitchen, she thought it might help to point out what daily life was like for Holt now.

"We've had to convert the dining room into a bedroom because the stairs are a problem—I'm sure you saw the wood we stuck over the porch steps as a makeshift ramp. There's that same thing down the back ones. But inside he'll need a stair lift for him to get to the second floor, and we haven't had a chance to install that yet—or figured out exactly when we'll be able to afford it."

Passing the downstairs bathroom to their left, she pointed to it. "We had to take the door off the bathroom so he could get the chair in there. Bridget— that's his wife—can help him on and off the toilet, but getting him in and out of the tub is a bigger deal. That takes muscle. That's why Yancy was here today. The nurse came to show him and Bridget how to help without doing any harm, but Holt really needs a different setup for that, too."

They reached the living room, and Marli pointed inside. "We've moved all the furniture against the walls to give him more space, but everywhere you see scratches on the walls or doorways means it's a tight fit for the chair—he even got it stuck trying to get into the mudroom this afternoon. So if you think he could go AWOL without a whole lot of trouble, you're wrong."

"I need to see that he's here," Dalton repeated implacably, giving no indication that he had any interest in what she was saying.

Marli knew Holt would appreciate not being pitied or tiptoed around by anyone—but particularly by the person who had been the target of his grievance since childhood. But she hoped to stir a bit of compassion in Dalton anyway. It just didn't seem as if she was succeeding.

They went through the kitchen to reach the double pocket doors that closed off the wide opening to the dining room.

Marli carefully slid the doors apart just enough for Dalton to see inside, where Holt was indeed sleeping in the king-size bed he and Bridget shared.

One glance and Dalton stepped back so she could close the doors again.

"Happy?" she asked, a hint of insolence creeping into her tone in spite of herself.

Dalton didn't give her the satisfaction of a response. He merely turned from her and retraced his steps back to the front door.

Following him, Marli reminded herself that snapping at him wouldn't be the right thing to do. Not for Holt. Dalton already had too many reasons to hold a grudge against him, and he had good reason to be acting this way.

So as he gained distance returning to the front of the house, she hurried to catch up and said, "Wait! Can we talk?"

He didn't answer and he didn't pause.

He was out the front door and so was she before she said, "Dalton! Please?"

He slowed down but took a few more steps before he stopped. Even then he didn't turn around. He left his back to her and she had the impression that he was fighting the urge to keep going.

Before the temptation to do that could gain ground, she said another "Please... Just hear me out..."

He finally did turn to face her but his expression was full of scorn and lacked any encouragement whatsoever.

Still, Marli said, "I know it's late in coming, but I owe you an apology. I really am sorry."

He cocked his head slightly, derisively quizzical. "For what, Marli?" he challenged, his tone filled with a horrible disdain for her. "Are you saying you did something wrong?"

"I know there's no apology big enough for just taking off the way I did and—"

"And it's just a hell of a coincidence that you're giving one *now*? Seventeen *years* after the fact? When your brother is on the verge of having his ass handed to him and you're hoping I'll go easy on him instead? Do you really think I'm dumb enough to believe that your paltry *sorry* isn't because of that?" He huffed. "Save it."

"I'm not saying I'm sorry because of Holt. I'm saying it because I owe it to you. I know what I did was bad, Dalton. I just didn't see any other options back then—"

"You didn't see any other options?" he parroted sarcastically. "Oh, yeah, because staying here for a couple of simple summer months before I left for Annapolis would have been torture. What would have happened if you'd stuck around, Marli?" Every time he said her name it was with a razor-sharp edge. "Did you think I'd do something to keep you from having all those *experiences* you needed to go out and have? Did you think I would stuff you in my duffel, take you with me and keep you under my bunk? Did you think I'd chain you up in the barn? Lock you in the shed—"

"Get me pregnant again…"

The words just slipped out. The moment they did, Marli regretted them. Especially when she saw the blow they struck and the increase in Dalton's fury.

"Oh, that was my fault was it? A torn condom the first time either of us had had sex and I was to blame?" he said in a tone that couldn't have been more harsh.

"No." Marli was quick to answer, shaking her head, seeing how badly this was going off the rails and wanting desperately to stop it. "It wasn't your fault. It wasn't my fault. It just happened…"

And standing there facing the most vivid reminder of it, the only person she'd ever let know that it had happened at all, brought with it a wave of the fear, the confusion, the agony and then the awful relief she'd silently, privately condemned herself for all these years. It washed over her like a tidal wave and as she weathered it, Dalton only made it worse.

"I took you to that goddamn clinic when the miscarriage started that day, scared out of my head that you might die, that maybe I should take you to an emergency room even though you said no. I sat in that waiting room in a cold sweat. You wouldn't say a word to me the whole way home from Billings afterward. And then that was it. You *left*. You left me hanging, not knowing if there were complications—if you were sick, bleeding to death. You wouldn't answer a stinking email and then I barely blinked and you were *gone*! And that was it? The last I ever saw or heard from you again as if I was nothing? As if we hadn't been anything…not friends or *anything*, since we were kids? As if we hadn't just gone through—"

"I know it was wrong," she said, tears in her throat. "I know it was awful. Hurtful. I know it—"

"It was a lousy, rotten thing to do. A lousy, rotten way to handle something that wasn't easy for me, either."

"But it was the *only* lousy, rotten thing I ever did to you," she reminded him in her own weak defense. "I always took your side when Holt was picking a fight or trying to take you down—"

"And then it was *you* who pulled the rug out from under me yourself!"

"Dalton—"

"You know what?" he said, shaking his head. "There's no point in arguing. It was a long time ago. It's over. There's no sense rehashing it. I'm here to do what I'm here to do, I guess you're here to do whatever you're here to do and that's it. I'll make my decision about your brother as I see fit, no matter what you do or say, no matter what you ever did or said. Just stay out of my way."

He turned his back to her once more and left her there in the yard, stunned by how deep his anger at her ran even now.

She tried to think of something to say to stop him, to make this better. Somehow.

But the only thing she could manage was one more feeble, beseeching "Dalton…"

And that didn't do it. If he heard it, he didn't acknowledge it; he just kept going.

As she watched him, she realized the tears that had been in her throat were blurring her eyes now.

Tears like so, so many she'd shed for months after she'd left here. Left him.

But it seemed like that was too long ago to cry over today. Maybe these tears were for Holt and the thought of his future being at the mercy of a man carrying such a deep grudge of his own.

Or maybe they were because she'd just seen how very much damage she'd done to someone she'd once loved with her whole heart.

Chapter Three

"Yeah, a lot has happened in a short amount of time."

"I can't believe it..." Dalton marveled as he took in the news from his brothers on Sunday morning. "All three of you are really out of or on your way out of the corps. You're all getting married and staying back in Merritt for good. Tanner even has a kid... I feel like I must have been out of touch for years instead of just the last few months."

"Like I said, a lot has happened in a short amount of time," Micah repeated as he heaved another case of beer into place.

Dalton, Quinn and Tanner had agreed to help Micah load a large refrigerated van with cases of beer from Micah's brewery. His line of craft beers was launching at the main Camden Superstore in Denver at the end of the week and his biggest delivery yet had to be made in advance. They'd used a forklift to bring pallets loaded with the cases outside, and now Quinn and Dalton were hoisting cases up to Micah and Tanner, who were in the bed of the truck to accept them.

"It's not completely out of the blue, though. There was some history to everything," Tanner said.

"So you better watch out," Quinn warned jokingly, "because here you are across the road from Marli Abbott again, and *no one* has history the way you have history with her."

"But he's thinking about court-martialing her brother," Micah said ominously.

"And she dumped him *hard* that last summer," Quinn added, not without some sympathy.

That was the only thing his family knew about the end of Dalton's relationship with Marli. As close as he'd always been to his brothers, he'd been closer to Marli from the time they'd first noticed each other until she'd disappeared on him. Because of that, when it came to her, there were many things he'd kept private. The pregnancy—and the miscarriage— had been their secret. The only thing his brothers knew was how shocked Dalton had been when Marli left and how desperate he'd been to contact her, how hard it had hit him that he'd never been able to.

"You were going over there last night when we left," Micah said then. "How'd that go?"

"I only went to make sure Holt hasn't gone AWOL. He was already asleep so it turned out to be nothing but a bed check and I came home," Dalton said, omitting the confrontation he and Marli had had. There was no need to let his brothers know about that—or about the fact that it had kept him up most of the night and was still dogging him today.

"So the two of you didn't butt heads?" Tanner asked.

Initially—because Marli was haunting his thoughts—Dalton thought Tanner was asking if he and Marli had butted heads. Then he realized his brother was referring to Holt—whom it was more common for Dalton to fight with.

"No," Dalton answered simply enough as he handed Micah a case of beer.

"Have the two of you seen each other since Syria?" This came from Quinn.

"No."

"Big Ben said he saw Holt," Tanner offered. "Shook him up to see him in a wheelchair. And that's permanent, huh?"

"It is," Dalton confirmed.

"The house over there is two floors. How's that working out with a chair?" Quinn asked.

"Not all that well from what I saw last night," Dalton answered, then he went on to relay what Marli had pointed out as she'd led him through the house.

"Is that where he'll land for good, though—in that house?" Another query from Micah. "I mean, even if he ends up court-martialed and in confinement, will he come back to live there after that, for the long haul?"

"That was my impression."

Micah's eyebrows arched. "I know it's Holt Abbott and he's never been a friend to any of us—"

"That's for sure," Quinn agreed. "And to Dalton he's been an all-out prick."

Micah went on, "And there's no excuse for disobeying an order, not to mention putting so many other people in harm's way..." He paused as if considering what he was about to say before saying it. "I wouldn't want to be in your shoes, Dalton, having to make the decision you have to make. If you decide to throw the book at Abbott I'm with you—I never had anyone in my command dumb enough to go against me. But on the other hand..." Micah still seemed reluctant to spell out whatever it was he was thinking. "It's got to be a tough adjustment to go from being an active duty marine to sleeping in a dining room, getting stuck in doorways, needing his wife to take him to the head and Yancy Coltrain to bathe."

No one argued with that. There was just silence and shrugs and nods that confirmed that Micah's opinion was shared by them all.

"He is still a marine," Micah continued. "And he was injured on a mission..."

"And he *is* one of Merritt's own..." Tanner said almost under his breath.

That couldn't be denied, either.

"You know…" Micah said unenthusiastically then. "This is right up the alley of the vets-helping-vets group working with me on this place."

"I always hear you call that group that. Does it have a real name?" Quinn asked.

"Nah. It's informal, just a bunch of guys, all resigned or retired military, who want to help other vets in any kind of bind. They have jobs, lives, families—they just volunteer their services. They talk about getting more organized but they never get around to it. They just go on doing what they can, when they can. But Abbott's situation is more in line with the reason they've gotten together than the repairs around here that they're helping me with. Abbott is in more genuine need."

"I would not want Clairy to have to help me use the head," Quinn said, also somewhat under his breath.

"And I know one of you guys would help me clean up the same way I'd help you, but damn, would I hate having to need that!" Tanner said.

"The group is set to come here on Tuesday," Micah said. He hesitated before adding in a resigned tone, "What I need done can wait. I could see if they'll work over at the Abbotts' instead…" He paused. "I'll leave it up to you, Dalton. Holt was brutal to you that whole last summer. Merciless. And even before that, if he could find a way to stick it to you, he did. Plus now…with the position he's put you in… None of us could blame you if you want to just court-martial him and then leave him to fend for himself when he gets out. Marine or not. One of Merritt's own or not."

"He sure as hell doesn't have any favors coming from you," Quinn said to Dalton.

"Not by a long shot," Tanner confirmed.

"And then there's Marli Abbott," Micah added. "You don't owe her anything, either."

"I'm doing my damnedest not to decide anything with her in mind at all," Dalton muttered.

But when it came to the idea of making anything easier for two people who had—each in their own way—made his life difficult? It was tempting to say they should have to deal with their issues on their own. Really tempting.

He didn't, though. Instead he said, "Let me think about the vets-helping-vets thing. For now, while you guys finish up these pallets, I'll go get that next load."

Dalton climbed behind the wheel of the forklift and drove it around to the rear of the old barn that housed the brewery. He was counting on his brothers moving on to a different topic of conversation by the time he got back to them with more cases of beer.

Unfortunately his own brain wasn't moving on— he was still thinking about Marli and that blowup the night before.

It had been ugly. And his reaction to her had bothered the hell out of him.

Actually, all of his reactions to her bothered the hell out of him—from the blistering anger he'd discovered in himself when he'd realized she was here, to an alarming combination of reactions to her in the course of the previous evening's argument.

He just didn't know where it was all coming from.

Yes, he'd gone through a rash of misery when she'd disappeared on him. But that was a lot of years ago, and time had put everything behind him—everything from their early childhood friendship to the first-love romance that had developed from it. Time had put behind him everything that had gone wrong to end their relationship, how she'd responded to that end and what she'd put him through with her silence.

His entire relationship with Marli had fallen into the category of things he'd experienced and learned from—no different than learning to ride a bicycle, learning to throw a football, learning to drive, learning to shave. She'd been his lesson in heartbreak. It was all part of the same thing—rites of passage into adulthood. Things to be experienced, learned from and then moved past. Nothing that should raise any kind of response in him now when faced with the source of the lesson.

Although…

He had to admit to himself that he did still have the first football he'd learned to throw and the first old-fashioned razor he'd shaved with. And that first car? There was still a picture of it in his wallet. They were all mementoes of those early lessons and he *did* have a reaction to them.

But they brought with them only fond memories.

Still, if Marli went into the category of life lessons, groundwork and rites of passage, then maybe it shouldn't come as any surprise that he'd had a reaction to her. Several of them.

It didn't mean he hadn't gotten over her. He didn't give two good goddamns about Marli Abbott. He'd gotten over her. Other women had come and gone—including one he'd almost married—and his years with Marli Abbott were nothing but time he'd spent that was long gone.

It was just the strength of his reactions to her that was weighing on him. He'd lost his temper big-time and that wasn't like him. He was well trained and experienced in unemotionally navigating any highly charged situation—the way the whole situation with the Abbotts was now. So why had he gotten so riled up last night?

He turned off the forklift, got out and went to load cases onto the pallet, thinking about just *how* riled up he'd been and trying to understand it.

It wasn't as if he hadn't worked it all out of his system—her and his feelings about what she'd done. Hell, he'd ranted and raved that whole summer seventeen years ago about her taking off without a word, about her ignoring his every attempt to reach her—to himself, to his brothers, to anyone who would listen. Then he'd gone to Annapolis accepting that everything between them was over and done with and thrown himself into the hardest choices he could make for four years to keep himself from thinking about her. And he'd topped that off with some heavy R and R drinking and partying to detox himself from her when there was a break. Until eventually he'd been able to forget about her.

So how was it possible that after all that—and after the passage of over a decade and a half—she'd struck such a nerve last night?

Maybe it wasn't so much that she'd struck a nerve as that last night was his first opportunity to have his say. That made some sense to him.

She'd shut him out so completely seventeen years ago that he hadn't gotten that opportunity, the way he should have. So maybe last night was just his overdue chance to air his side and get some things off his chest. True, it had erupted in a surprising fury. But that's what happened when something pent-up needed a release. Even if he hadn't been aware that there *was* anything pent-up.

But the good thing about that, he decided, was now that he *had* vented whatever lingering ire there had been, it genuinely and fully *was* out of his system. The volcano had blown, spewed whatever lava had been left in the bottom of it and now it was completely defunct.

The more he considered that idea, the more reasonable an explanation it seemed and the more under control he felt. That one big reaction to her was spent. Over with.

That was called closure, wasn't it?

He liked that thought. That shouting match last

night might have been a big finish but it was a finish nonetheless. And that meant that now he really could move on. He could relegate Marli Abbott to the same status she'd had for the last seventeen years—the long distant past.

He breathed a deep sigh of relief and got back into the forklift, maneuvered it into position, lifted the next pallet with it and reversed direction to get out from behind the brewery.

And it was in that moment that, for no reason, Marli slipped into his mind again. Marli and the smaller reactions he'd had to her even in the midst of being supremely pissed off.

Seeing her again was weird. And during the argument it had been as if he'd volleyed back and forth through time.

Standing there face-to-face with her, he hadn't been able to keep from seeing what a knockout woman she'd become. Then he'd flashed back to how she'd looked when she was a little girl, a bigger girl, a teenager blossoming into the almost woman he'd last known her as. The almost woman he hadn't ever been able to get his fill of looking at. Staring at. Daydreaming about.

Definitely weird.

One minute last night she was someone badgering him to hear her out, and when he had, suddenly, he was flashing back to arguments they'd had before. Reminders that she didn't shy away or back down from anything. That she was outspoken, straightforward, even in admitting her own wrongdoing. That she made no excuses. That she played no games. Reminders of those things he'd liked about her when he was ten. And twelve. And thirteen and fourteen and…all along. Those things he'd still had to give some involuntary respect to last night—another of those reactions he hadn't wanted to have.

But involuntary respect wasn't really anything, right? It wasn't anywhere near attraction to her, he assured himself as he slowly guided the forklift from the rear of the brewery. Even if that involuntary respect had caused him to think that there was still more to her than to any other woman he'd encountered since her.

Again, it was just some weird mingling of the past and the present.

But there had been something else, too, a small unwelcome voice said from the recesses of his mind. Something else that had been eating at him that he didn't want to think about.

From the time they were kids, when they'd been at odds with each other, the simple sound of her voice had been enough to cut through the mad in him.

And of all the things that had changed about her, her voice was the same.

So last night there had been momentary flickers—no more than split seconds—when the sound of her voice had threatened to do that again…

He'd almost instantly returned to his righteous anger. But still…

"She's not going to get to me," he said under the drone of the forklift's engine.

She wasn't going to get to him because it was the old Marli who had. The old Marli he'd been so sure he knew. But after the way she'd left? He'd had to accept that he'd been wrong—he hadn't really known her at all.

The van came into view with his three brothers sitting in the back of it, legs dangling, waiting for him.

The sight of them helped bring him firmly into the present once more. Firmly *out* of his thoughts about the previous evening's encounter with Marli Abbott.

He was glad for that. Because it cemented in him the knowledge that he and Marli Abbott had run their course as a couple—right to an end that wasn't good for anyone. And now it was far, far behind him and the only thing he needed to focus on was what to do about her brother.

He could just go back to forgetting about her the way he'd finally forgotten about her years ago.

"Where've you been?" Micah criticized when he reached the van where the other pallet was unloaded.

"Hey, I'm a one-man operation here," he answered.

But even as he returned to work and the banter of his brothers, that small unwelcome voice in his head sounded again, telling him something else he didn't want to hear…

That maybe he'd never completely forgotten about Marli Abbott at all…

* * *

"I never thought it'd be so nice to sit on this old porch and eat pie," Holt said with a replete sigh. "And tell me my wife doesn't make the best one you've ever tasted, Marli."

"The best," Marli agreed, taking her own empty dessert dish and those of her brother and sister-in-law to bring into the kitchen.

It was after nine o'clock on Sunday night. Because the evening air was cool and pleasant, Marli, Bridget and Holt had gone out onto the front porch to enjoy the truly delectable cherry pie Bridget had made.

The local nurse had come again to check in on Holt that morning and had decreed that he was doing well. Marli, Holt and Bridget had used the afternoon for unpacking and settling in, and then Bridget and Marli had made an old-fashioned pot roast for Sunday supper. All in all Bridget and Holt seemed to have had a great day and Marli was happy to see her brother in such good spirits.

She couldn't say the same for herself. Not since she and Dalton had had it out the night before.

She put the rinsed plates in the dishwasher, her mind still caught on Dalton and that fight.

Over the years she'd wondered how it might go if she met up with him again, but she'd never imagined it like that. It weighed on her—and not only for Holt's sake.

Despite the end of her time with Dalton, despite her full knowledge that he had every right and reason to be furious with her, the depth of his anger had still come as a shock.

All these years she'd carried with her the guilt of what she'd done. She'd had no doubt that it was as hard on him to be left behind as it had been for her to leave and sever all ties and communication with him. But still, in her mind when she'd pictured facing him again, it had played out the way disagreements long ago had. Back then, regardless of what kind of rift had ever developed between them, they'd always forgiven each other and come back around to the closeness they'd shared. There hadn't been any lingering spite or malice.

But obviously those days were over. Now she and Dalton were less than strangers to each other. And Holt wasn't the only one holding on to bitterness and resentment and hard feelings.

She closed the dishwasher and stood in the empty kitchen, staring into space and lost in her own thoughts.

This wasn't how she wanted things to be. In fact, she was surprised by just how much it hurt to know that Dalton felt the way he felt now. Even if Holt was taken out of the equation and there was no potential jeopardy to him attached, she just couldn't bear that there was so much bad blood between her and someone who had—even if it *was* once upon a time—been so important to her.

Because Dalton *had* been important to her. Her memories of him before the pregnancy devastation were only good, treasured memories. And she just couldn't let that bad ending define everything.

But was it even possible for her to somehow make things right with him now?

She hadn't gotten very far last night with an apology.

And like last night, any attempt she made to regain old ground between them would make him suspect that she was only doing it to get him to go easy on Holt.

"What a mess you made, Marli," she whispered to herself, so, so regretting the way things with Dalton were now.

That regret brought with it the image of him from the night before to torment her—the icy contempt in those remarkable Camden blue eyes, the fierceness of the expression on that male masterpiece of a face…

Not that his turning out to be one of the best-looking men she'd ever seen was even part of the reason she wanted to make things better between them…

Was it?

No, of course it wasn't. The ground she wanted to regain with Dalton was just friendship ground. Nothing but friendship ground. The fact that he was handsome as all get-out didn't make an iota of difference.

Especially when she was still stinging from her third—*third*—broken engagement and she was determined to steer clear of any more relationships until she figured out exactly how and where and to what extent a man ever *would* fit into her life.

So no, it definitely didn't matter what kind of physical specimen Dalton was—or any other man at this point. Men were off-limits for her for the time being. She was committed to that. Even if she couldn't seem to commit to actually getting to the altar.

But the friendship she'd had with Dalton? That had sustained her through so much—difficulties at home, her mother's depression after the scandal with her parents' divorce, the scrapes her brother had gotten into when the chip on his shoulder had led him into trouble. Dalton's support through all that, his acceptance of her in every other way, had gotten her through it. Having him find positives in her and the things she did when other people had only seen negatives had meant everything to her.

Even recalling it gave her a touch of longing to have some of that unconditional acceptance back in her life now. She needed it more than ever after the blowup in Denver that had ended her work partnership and her last engagement. The blowup had happened so close to when Holt was injured that she hadn't had time to process it completely and was just beginning to now. The blowup that had found her flawed and to blame. By two people at once…

Not that she had illusions that she and Dalton might get anywhere near to him offering her any kind of solace.

But still she genuinely did want to do *something* to get them on better terms. She just didn't know what.

When they were kids she would have been able to make things right with an extra cookie stashed for him in her lunch. Or giving up her prized water-skipping rock. Or inviting him on an adventure. Or warning him of some trick or dirty deed Holt was planning against him. Or offering him her notes for a class he'd missed.

Or accompanying an apology with some flirting that would lead to making out…

No, no, no, she wasn't going *there*, she reprimanded herself, dialing it back when her mind went one step too far.

But since she didn't think a cookie or a water-skipping rock would help the situation with Dalton now, she knew she was going to have to come up with something else. She didn't know if it would help to keep up the apologies and remorse until they wore him down, but she definitely intended to do that. Even if his only response was open scorn. Maybe just letting him air that scorn again and again would eventually help get rid of it so they could move past it. And if that meant that she had to be his verbal punching bag, then so be it.

But she *was* going to persist. She wasn't going to just sit back and accept that Dalton hated her now. She wasn't going to let his stubborn anger at her fester any more than it already had. The way Holt's anger at the Camdens had since he was a child.

She might not have handled the breakup with Dalton well, but even in retrospect she believed that their going their separate ways seventeen years ago had been the best thing for them both. Now she just had to deal with the downside of the choice she'd made. Regardless of what that might mean.

Better late than never, she told herself.

And at least now she wasn't a young, hormonal, love-struck teenager at risk of forgetting herself just from one glimpse of him, one reach of his hand for hers, one for-her-alone glint in his eye.

"Marli? Are you coming back out? Could you bring Holt a glass of water?" Bridget called in to her, pulling Marli out of her musings.

"Sure," she answered, taking a glass from the cupboard to fill from a pitcher.

She was headed outside with the water when suddenly she heard a different tone coming from the porch: Holt's voice raised loud and rancorous, sounding as if he was spoiling for a fight.

"Oh, here comes *Major* Camden to say I told you so."

Marli moved faster out the door, and she found Dalton on his way up the porch steps—the recipient of Holt's comment.

Once more he was wearing casual clothes—camo-colored utility pants and a tan crew neck T-shirt that displayed mammoth muscles. But his stance was still all-military and no-nonsense—as was the expression on his face and the tone of his voice.

"I saw you out here so I decided now was as good a time as any to give you an update on your current status. It might be better if we speak privately."

"My wife and my sister can hear whatever you have to say to me," Holt stated derisively.

"Please be nice, honey," Bridget begged quietly.

"To Camden?" Holt huffed as if she was delusional.

"Holt…" Marli added her own rebuke.

But her brother ignored it.

"Just spit it out," he said, sneering at Dalton. "Did you come to tell me you're bringing me up on charges?"

Dalton remained formal and reserved but clearly in command as he informed them of how Holt's actions had angered both a senator and a colonel. "The senator has taken political heat that he's afraid will hurt his chance for reelection. Colonel Lundquist thinks that you made him look bad and he's pushing for a court-martial. He sent me here to make that decision now that you're well enough to answer for your actions."

"And I'm sure there's nothing you'd like more than to make him happy at my expense," Holt accused hotheadedly. "You have to be thrilled that not only will I never have the chance to gain equal—or superior—rank to you, but now you can even make sure I'm *dis*honorably discharged."

Marli saw that he was deliberately antagonizing Dalton. But still Dalton didn't lose his temper. Instead, in a cool, unquestionably controlled tone, he warned, "And you realize that if I have you court-martialed the way the colonel wants and you're convicted and dishonorably discharged, you'll lose your benefits—including the disability compensation that would give you an income and cover all or most of your medical care."

"Yeah, I know what you can do to me. But if you think I'll ever beg for mercy from you, think again. You can stick it right—"

"Oh, Holt, stop!" Marli snapped. Holt never knew when to cut his losses, but she wasn't going to let him make his situation even worse.

"He already knows he's got me where he wants me," Holt said to her. "He's going to do whatever the hell he pleases, and I'm not groveling to get him to do anything else."

"I wouldn't expect you to," Dalton said. "I just thought you should know—"

"Where I *stand*?" Holt sneered.

"I thought you should know the damage you've done to your career, so you can be prepared for the consequences," Dalton said flatly. "And if you have any defense for disobeying my orders, now would be the time to give it."

"My *defense* is what I told you at the time—that should have been *my* mission. I'd done the recon, I knew the area—"

"Not well enough." Dalton stated the obvious.

The rage that remark raised in Holt was almost palpable in the evening air. "Get the hell off my porch!" he shouted childishly, apparently having no better comeback.

Dalton was still composed. "If that's all you have to say—"

"One more thing—I'd rather end up in the brig than ever taking orders from *you* again!"

"Good to know," Dalton countered, then left as abruptly as he'd arrived.

"Sometimes you're your own worst enemy." Marli shot the words at her brother, leaving him to his wide-eyed and obviously alarmed wife while Marli went after Dalton, hoping to be able to do some kind of damage control.

He was at the end of the driveway when she caught up to him. "Dalton!" she called much as she had the evening before, expecting no better response from him than he'd given then.

But this time he stopped and turned to her without the need for more entreaties. Not that his expression was any less cold.

"I won't discuss this with you. You don't have any more part in a military investigation than a stranger on the street," he said, giving no latitude.

"Okay…" she tentatively conceded, still taken aback by his curtness toward her. But keeping in mind that she had reasons of her own to speak with

Dalton, she persevered, "But could we talk anyway? Maybe take a walk?"

He wasn't quick to answer, which Marli thought was a good sign. It seemed to her that a refusal would come with some speed. Unless, like the evening before, his fury just needed a minute to mount...

She braced for that possibility, reminding herself that she was going to take whatever he dished out.

But rather than unloading any more venom on her, he said, "I do have something I should probably tell you..."

He didn't sound happy about whatever it was but he also didn't sound ominous or angry. She decided she'd even take chilly, aloof civility without complaint. It was still preferable to what he'd spewed last night.

"Okay," she said again, this time with more vigor.

They set out on the dark country road they'd walked together innumerable times. Without more preamble, Dalton launched into what he had to say. "Micah has connections with a group of veterans— he calls them vets-helping-vets because that's who they are and what they do. It's nothing formal, just volunteers pitching in as needed. When I told him what's going on with your house not being fully wheelchair accessible, he called one of those guys and explained the situation. They're willing to come in and help with renovations—build ramps, expand doorways, put up rails in the bathrooms... Apparently there's even a stair lift someone donated to them that's available and they can install it—"

That was the last thing Marli had expected to hear and she could hardly believe it. "No kidding?"

"Like I said, it's all volunteer, no charge for labor or materials—they've all apparently been donated to the cause, too. Micah says the cleanup and a lot of the detail work and finish will be left undone, like trim, painting and patching, but otherwise—"

Marli jumped at the offer. "I can paint and patch. Oh, that would help so much!" she said, thinking how like Dalton it was to offer something like this, even if it was coming in the unpleasantly formal new-Dalton tone. "Thank you!"

"Don't thank me. This is Micah's doing and the group he knows. I'm only relaying the message."

But he *was* relaying it. "You could have left the help for someone who doesn't have a dishonorable discharge hanging over his head but you didn't— that's something."

"In this I'm separating who your brother is and what he's done, and considering only that he *is* still a marine. For now, at least."

"Thank you anyway. And yes, we will *gladly* accept. No matter what happens, this is Holt's home, and this will make such a difference for him and Bridget. She and I weren't sure how we were going to do it ourselves or afford to pay to get it done. And the stair lift? We were afraid it might be years before we could get one of those."

Dalton had no reaction to her effusive gratitude as they made the U-turn they'd always made at *their* tree and headed back toward their houses.

"And you wanted to talk to me about what?" he asked then, all business.

She wasn't exactly sure what to say but she leaped in anyway. "For one thing, I'm sorry for the way Holt just acted."

She wanted to put Holt's bad behavior in context in case Dalton had lost sight of it. "He's always been a jackass when it comes to you. You know that he's always had it in for you because of what your mother did all those years ago…"

Raina Camden had been a unique—and difficult—woman. In an effort to ensure that her sons were tough and ambitious, she'd been incredibly hard on them to make them into what she saw as "real" men. She'd trained them never to take a back seat to anyone or accept anything less than success. She'd drilled into them not to hold back, to do whatever it took to get what they wanted.

Raina had been just as determined to be strong and formidable herself and when Marli's father—mayor of Merritt at the time—had courted a Camden Superstore for the town, it had set her off.

Raina had resented mightily that her branch of the Camden family—descendants of Hector Camden who was Ben's father —had not shared in the success of Hector's brother H.J., founder of the wildly successful Camden Superstores. There was no way she was going to tolerate having a superstore built right under her nose or those other Camdens prospering even more from the spending of her town.

She'd decided to run against Owen Abbott for mayor, and she'd run an incredibly dirty campaign, including hiring private investigators to dig up dirt both on Owen himself and on what he had promised in order to attract a superstore.

That was how it came out that the then mayor and father of seven-year-old Marli and eight-year-old Holt was having an affair with a woman in the next county.

It was also revealed that the guarantees Owen had made to secure a superstore risked bankrupting Merritt.

Raina had leaked the news openly, making no attempt to disguise her actions. Her unscrupulousness had cost her the election but had so soured the town's opinion of Owen that he'd lost, too, leaving the victory to a third candidate. Plus, the revelations about Owen's affair had caused the end of Owen's marriage to Ginger.

Owen had already had a drinking problem—which Raina had also highlighted during the campaign. After he'd lost the election, his marriage and family, and ultimately his mistress, too, his drinking problem had only gotten worse. A year after Owen left office, he was killed in a car accident while driving drunk.

Holt had developed an intense anger and resentment toward and hatred of the Camdens in general, overlooking that his father's actions were at all to blame for his situation.

Holt hadn't focused his rage specifically on Dalton until Marli had become friends with him not long after Owen's death. Then all of her brother's animosity had been aimed at Dalton and that was how it remained.

"You know Holt just made you the target of his grudge, and he can't seem to keep himself from acting on it," Marli reminded. "It's irrational but when it comes to anything to do with you, the anger takes over, leading to bad decisions—including the one he made in Syria."

"So you admit that it was a bad decision to ignore my orders?"

"Of course it was. Just like when he used to sabotage your football gear and your basketball shoes to make you lose games even though he didn't actually want our school to lose. Or when he'd screw with your test so you'd get a zero, even knowing that *he'd* end up with a zero, too—they were *all* bad decisions. This one was on a bigger scale but it was still a decision fueled by his grudge. Only I wasn't there to warn you or try to stop him."

"That doesn't matter to the senator or the colonel. And I'm not discussing the investigation with you."

"I'm just saying that *you* know that's why he does what he does when you're involved—even on that scale—and why he was just such a big-mouth jerk to you now. I don't think he can help himself. And I don't want to see you holding that same kind of grudge and turning into him."

Dalton's head pivoted in her direction, and when Marli glanced sideways at him, she found his eyebrows arched high. "Your brother has always made himself a thorn in my side, but I'm not carrying a grudge toward him. What he's pulled has a tendency to backfire and this time—"

"I'm not talking about you having a grudge against him. I'm talking about you having one against *me*. Because last night—"

"Last night I didn't say anything to you that you didn't have coming."

"I know. And I agree—I did have it coming. But the thing is, if you don't accept my apology, if you don't recognize that I truly am sorry for what I did, if you just walk away and keep being mad at me and hating me and never letting us move on from it, then your justified anger turns into a grudge. Just like with Holt."

Dalton turned his face forward again, shaking his head as if he could shake off her words. "What do you want from me, Marli?"

"I want you to let me have it—yell and scream at me until there's nothing left in you to yell and scream so we can—"

"Go back?" he asked facetiously. "Be what? Friends again? More than friends again? Because that's not going to happen. Seventeen years ago you showed me that I never really knew you at all. I'm not going back to blindly trusting you now that I know better. I didn't know who you were then, I sure as hell don't know who you are now and that's how it is."

"You *did* know me then."

"The person I *thought* you were wouldn't have done to me what you did," he said flatly, obstinately.

"So you don't want to get past this. You *want* to be like Holt."

"I'm nothing like your brother."

"You're refusing to see anything but your own injured point of view—that's Holt. And look where it's gotten him."

"Your brother is unreasonable. He has his grudge aimed at someone who never did a thing to him, who was a kid the same way he was when it all went down. I'm angry at you for *your* actions and no one else's. You proved that you're not someone I can trust ever again. I'm not out to do you any harm. I just don't want—"

"You knew better than anyone that I would do anything to get out of here—"

"Not like that. Not acting as if I was what you had to run like hell from."

"You *were* what I had to run like hell from," she admitted. "But you should have known why—"

"Apparently to get away from me. You had to run far and fast and undercover—like I was your damn enemy or stalker or something—and then you had to stay hidden. Well, mission accomplished. You got what you wanted, which appears to have been me out of your life. I just don't know what you want from me now."

"To start over?" she suggested. It was clear that rehashing the past wasn't going to get her anywhere.

"To start over," he parroted. "With what end in mind?"

There was no question that he thought she was doing this so he'd lighten up on Holt.

"No end in mind," she said. "Just having back someone in my life who was important to me, who knew me in ways no one else ever did or ever has. We used to mean so much to each other. I think we should at least try to…make peace…"

"We're not at war. You used your own methods to go your way. I went mine. At this point there's no more to it."

"Except that you've gone your way carrying a grudge—just like Holt," she reminded him.

Dalton didn't say anything for a long time—but he didn't turn back and end their walk, not even when they reached the house. Instead Dalton kept going—something he wouldn't have done if he'd wanted to end this here and now, which gave her a glimmer of hope.

So Marli just went on walking, too, giving him time to think.

But after a way farther down the street in silence he sighed and said, "I still don't trust your motives. What do you *really* want?"

"I want us not to be at odds. I want to know how you are, *who* you are now, what you've done, where you've been. I'm just curious about how life has worked out for you, for someone who has a place in my memories that no one else has. I want what we were to each other before not to just be trashed..."

She expected him to again launch into how she bore the responsibility for that.

But after another moment's pause he said, "Say we do that, that we aren't *at odds*. Where would that leave us? As acquaintances again? I might have to go harder on your brother to prove that my connection to you doesn't have any influence."

"Well, I don't want that," Marli said in frustration. She couldn't tell if he was just being particularly contrary or if he was testing her. He'd never been this difficult to persuade before—which seemed to make it clear just how negative his feelings toward her were.

They'd reached an equal distance from their houses in the opposite direction of *their* tree and took the other U-turn they'd taken before.

"Are you just telling me that you don't want to fix this?" she asked forlornly. While she was willing to take more heat from him in order to reach better ground between them, not even her usual tenacity could let her persist if it meant things could go even worse for Holt.

Still, Dalton didn't give her an immediate answer.

Only after several more yards did he warn, "It won't gain your brother any points."

"That's fine," she conceded. "My only defense of him is what I've already given anyway. His grudge against you makes him stupid and gives him a big mouth and usually backfires—like it did this time. But if you and I burying the hatchet won't cost him any additional points, then I'd still like to give it a try."

"And if I ultimately court-martial him?"

Another test.

Okay, I get it—you really don't trust me...

But Marli recognized that she'd earned that. It was just something else she would have to be patient with.

"If it has to come to a court-martial, that will have to be between the two of you—the way it always was when I couldn't head things off." But at least if she and Dalton could regain some semblance of friendship, she would know that Holt wasn't being punished for a grudge Dalton was holding against her. Holt's consequences would be his own and his own alone.

"I really won't talk any more about the situation with your brother—if you think becoming my confidante will give you an opening to spy, you'll be disappointed."

"I've said my piece about it," she reiterated, keeping it simple. "The subject will be off-limits."

Silence came again and she knew he was weighing whether or not to believe her. She also knew she *would* need to avoid trying to sway him because the minute she said anything else in defense of Holt, she would trigger Dalton's distrust once more and that would be that—she'd be right back to worrying that Holt might have to pay for her crimes against Dalton.

Then, out of the blue, he said, "What do you want to know?"

His tone was neutral rather than friendly, but Marli was willing to take whatever she could get from him. "I don't even know if you're married or… divorced…or engaged… Or maybe you have five kids…" She ended that in a softer tone because it seemed to touch on that sore spot in their shared history.

"Not married. Never married, so not divorced. Or currently engaged," he said succinctly. "And since it isn't as if your brother and I have beers and catch up when our paths cross—I don't know any of those things about you, either."

He didn't sound genuinely interested but she answered anyway. "Not married. Never married, so not divorced," she echoed his words. "But I have been engaged…three times…" she said sheepishly.

"*Three* times?"

She wasn't thrilled that that was what got a genuine reaction out of him, but at least the reaction seemed to have some dry humor to it.

"Sad to say," she admitted.

"Are you engaged now?"

"No. Three times engaged, three broken engagements," Marli confessed. And because she didn't want to get into it any deeper than that, she returned to the even more vulnerable subject and said, "So no marriage, no kids for me. You?"

"No."

They both left another moment of silence, maybe for the baby they might have had together, maybe not.

Then, to get beyond it—and still feeling a need to find out if there was any notable relationship in his life—she said, "How about a girlfriend? A significant other you live with?"

"No," he said, giving her more relief than she knew she should have felt. "Is there someone you're on the way to engagement number four with?"

"Nooo," she answered firmly. "Broken engagement number three happened just before Holt was hurt, and since then Bridget and I have been going wherever he's needed surgeries and treatments. Bridget needed the moral support and I wanted to treat Holt, too—"

"Are you a doctor?"

"I have a PhD in Chinese medicine—acupuncture, acupressure, herbs…"

"Where did that come from?" he asked in surprise.

"It came from trying to find something that would help my mom," she explained. "It turned out that she wasn't just down in the dumps because Merritt was a bad place and she felt stuck and stifled, or because her marriage and the way it ended made her unhappy—all the things she always blamed and preached to me about. After…"

Marli hesitated, unsure if she should get into this territory again. But now that she'd begun, she didn't know how to detour out of it. "After you took me to the clinic in Billings and I went home, my mom got a call from her sister in Los Angeles. Aunt Annie had gotten hurt at work and needed help. She asked Mom to come to L.A. I…" Oh, such sensitive territory… "I talked Mom into letting me go, too, and then—once we were there—I lobbied for her to let me live with Aunt Annie. Mom decided maybe it was time for a fresh start for herself and chose to stay, too.

"But even with that fresh start in a big city, Mom was still miserable all the time. It actually took a half-hearted suicide attempt for her to be diagnosed with clinical depression. But the counseling and the meds never got her completely out of it and I kept looking for something that might—"

"Acupuncture?" he said as if she'd told him she'd set out to help her mother with magic potions.

Marli was just glad he was focused more on that than on what she'd had to revisit to get there. "Acupuncture," she confirmed.

"Did it help?"

"It did. And without the side effects the meds had had on her. It didn't turn her into a lighthearted person, but it helped even her out and that was a win."

"Is it still working for her?" he said with a skepticism Marli was accustomed to facing. Alternative medicines didn't get a lot of respect.

"It helped until she died two years ago in a freeway accident."

"I'm sorry. I didn't know…"

"I know," Marli assured him, finding a small comfort in hearing a condolence from him.

"And now you're back in Merritt to stay?"

There was an edge of accusation in his voice that she chose to ignore. "All those years of hearing my mom talk about how horrible this small town was, how many better places there were, how much better life would be outside of here—and believing it—"

"Which was why you were hell-bent on getting out," he reminded her with more of that edge.

"Your mother hammered it into you to always come out on top. Mine hammered into me that Merritt and getting married young were horrible traps that would ruin my life the way it had ruined hers. She had me convinced I'd be doomed if I *wasn't* hell-bent on getting out."

Dalton acknowledged that with a raise of his chin but no more.

Marli went on. "By the time she died, I'd had the chance to live in a lot of non-small-town places, meet a lot of people, have a lot of experiences—"

"Experiences," he repeated goadingly. "God did I get sick of that word."

She chose not to let him provoke her now that she'd come this far. "Well, after all that, I realized that big cities left me feeling lonely in a way I never did here. That I missed being part of a community that was just one big extended family. That I hadn't been able to find the kind of loyalty I'd had here..."

It felt as if she was saying too much, so she wrapped it up. "I realized that in comparison—and from my own perspective instead of my mother's skewed viewpoint—Merritt had been kind of a nice little place to live. It appealed to me to come home to it. I'd set the wheels into motion to do it, just when Holt was hurt."

"And now that you're here, you're staying?"

"I am."

They'd reached their houses again and this time Dalton did stop.

But Marli was unexpectedly unwilling to let him go yet, so she went on talking. "I was going to live in the house but now I'm in the cottage instead. I rented an office on Independence and I've filed for my business license. This is it—I'm here to stay."

"Never thought I'd see that."

"Me neither."

The expression on his handsome face was inde-cipherable and once again she was left taking in all the ways he'd changed—the physical alterations that were to the good, and the new distance between them that she hoped to erase.

That might not ever change, she told herself, try-ing to accept it.

And yet still she couldn't help wishing that it would.

That he would maybe find a way to forgive her.

That he would look at her, talk to her, the way he had when he'd liked her.

Wishing for any amount of warmth in those blue eyes. For less stiffness in his stance. Less stiltedness in his voice and attitude.

Wishing that having a simple conversation with him wasn't like pulling teeth.

Wishing for the days when they would have stayed in that spot talking and talking because they never got enough of that. Never got enough of each other's company. Never got enough of each other.

Wishing for the days when they only stopped talking so that they could start kissing…

Marli snapped herself out of that thought, which had come on its own, without invitation. It was silly and pointless to think about that, since there was no chance anything like that would happen between them now.

Then, proving just how eager he was to get away from her, he simply told her that the vets-helping-vets people would come on Tuesday.

"I really do appreciate that. I'll make sure we're all ready for them so nothing is in the way and they can just dig in."

Dalton nodded and she expected that to be the end of it.

But for another moment he went on looking at her before he said, "I'm not holding a grudge."

She almost smiled at his need to continue that protest but decided to just accept the statement. "Good."

"It took me a while but eventually I saw that things worked out the way they should have. We both had things to do, growing up to do... In Merritt we were wrapped in a cocoon together and we had to bust out of it. If we hadn't, it probably would have strangled us. Both of us."

Marli nodded, agreeing despite how painful it had been to emerge from that cocoon.

Then he said, "But I'm not sure how it would have been for me if you'd said you were married now... with kids..."

That seemed like a very big disclosure.

"I don't know how it would have been for me, either...if that was how things were with you..." she whispered.

He stared at her a second longer, then said goodnight.

"Good night," she answered, trying not to entertain too much hope.

For what, she didn't know.

But his telling her it would have bothered him to hear that she was married or had kids felt like he'd shown her the barest hint of the person she'd formerly known.

And she couldn't deny that it would make her happy to see more of it...

Chapter Four

"I'm tired and we need to be up and out of here so early tomorrow morning. Holt, let's go to bed."

It was ten o'clock Monday night and after a long day of prepping the house for construction, Marli, Bridget and Holt had again ended up on the front porch for the last slices of Bridget's cherry pie. Once they'd finished eating, the Nordic beauty stood up to gather the empty plates and urge her husband to end the day.

"What time do you guys need to be in Billings tomorrow?" Marli asked.

"The appointment is at nine thirty. We're gonna leave here by seven so we have plenty of time," Holt answered.

Her brother was scheduled for physical therapy.

"I keep telling him that it's less than an hour's drive to Billings, but you know how he is—he always wants to be early and I never drive fast enough for him. Luckily there's a diner across the street from the office so once we get there we can have breakfast until the appointment. At least I won't have to make anything but coffee before we go."

"Even Marli thinks you drive too slow," Holt teased his wife.

"I do not," Marli countered.

The couple headed for the door.

"Are you coming in?" Bridget asked.

"I think I'll sit out here a little longer," she answered. "Be careful tomorrow and have a good time."

The drive and the treatment tired Holt. In order to keep it from being too much of a strain, and also in order to stay out of the way of the work that needed to be done, Marli had encouraged them to get a hotel room and make the return trip on Wednesday. It was the first time since Holt had been hurt that he was well enough for them to have a small romantic getaway, so they were splurging on a fancy resort where Holt would rest after his therapy while Bridget had a massage. They also had reservations at a nice restaurant.

"Thanks for today and overseeing tomorrow," her sister-in-law said as she and Holt went inside.

"No problem. See you on Wednesday when you get back," Marli called after them. "Oh, but hey, will you turn off the porch light? It's attracting mosquitos."

The light went off, leaving Marli alone in the dark, in the peace and quiet of the summer night.

And staring at the Camden house.

There was no good reason for her to focus on the place. Except maybe that her eyes might as well be on the same thing her mind had been on all last night and through the entire day today.

Not that she was thinking about the big, beautiful steeply roofed two-story country-style structure that dwarfed the nondescript Abbott farmhouse. No, it was a particular occupant whom she couldn't get out of her head.

She'd realized when she'd decided to move home to Merritt that there would be a lot of memories of Dalton. Good sentimental memories mostly, full of nostalgia.

But their encounters since his arrival had been totally lacking in sentiment or nostalgia. When she thought about him now, she didn't think about the past—she thought about all the issues with the present…and the way she responded to the person that he was now.

If he wasn't here he would still just be the cute teenage boy from her past. He wouldn't be the tall, broad-shouldered, well-muscled man with the face of a cologne model.

And she was only human. Even if she'd never known him before, never been attracted to him before, never had feelings for him before, one look at the guy would have made her take notice. The same way Bridget had. Or anyone would. A man who looked like that didn't cross any woman's path without turning heads.

But she *had* known him before—had cared about him and had chemistry with him—so maybe that was why his new appearance was impacting her so much. Maybe that was why it was impossible for her not to picture him in her mind's eye every minute of the day and night. Impossible not to sneak peeks at the Camden house every time she passed a window just in case he might be in sight.

If not for their old connection, then maybe she would have been able to simply note that he was hot—the way Bridget had—and leave it at that. But that wasn't an option for her.

And if it wasn't difficult enough, toss in the current dynamics between them and that just made things worse. One minute she was lost in the image of him and trying to calm the subsequent flutters in her stomach, and the next she was feeling guilty and remorseful and couldn't bear the idea that he had such horrible thoughts and feelings about her now.

It was a confusing cocktail that was messing with her mind, her emotions, her sleep and her concentration. She didn't know what to do about it, how to handle it or how to make it stop.

And when fatigue had had her in its grip last night in bed and the image of Dalton was so vividly haunting her, she hadn't been able to keep herself from wondering what it might be like to kiss the grown-up Dalton. If it would be different. As good. Not as good. As improved as his face and body...

Not that she'd ever have the chance to find out.

When it came to Dalton Camden there was nothing but the past for her. A past that had burned him, scarred him. Whatever attraction she felt for him, it couldn't possibly be mutual. Not when he was so certain that he could never trust her again. There just didn't seem to be any way to heal that rift.

Even if she tried to be absolutely open and honest with him, she doubted that he'd believe her. And she wasn't sure she would be able to handle making herself that vulnerable anyway.

When it came to the Dalton-of-the-past, she'd always been open and honest with him. She'd let him see her every vulnerability. Until that awful end.

But exposing herself in that way wasn't something she'd done with anyone since the day she'd left him. It wasn't something she'd done in any of her relationships, actually—romantic or even with friends. It was one of the things that her last fiancé Arnie and her officemate Alice had dinged her for eight months ago.

And to do it now, with the Dalton-of-today? That seemed risky.

It was all just so convoluted and complex and confusing and complicated now.

Oh, there he is...

His childhood bedroom was in the front upstairs corner of the house. And suddenly she spotted him standing at a window there.

She couldn't see him in any great detail but the mere outline of those shoulders almost broke her out into a sweat.

Was he looking over at her house, thinking about her the way she was thinking about him?

He was probably just looking out at the night, she told herself.

But if he *was* looking at her house, could he see her there on the porch?

If he could, would he come over like he would have in the old days?

And what was wrong with her that that idea gave her a tiny charge?

She reminded herself that if he came over it would probably only be to blast her again.

But still she sat up straighter with anticipation. She took stock of what she had on, of how her hair was behaving, wishing she'd bothered with mascara...

And she asked herself if she should tell him how wrong he was in thinking that she'd left because she *hadn't* cared about him...

He didn't stand at the window long before he yanked down the shade as if he was angry with it. And even though Marli remained on the alert and waiting, he never did come outside.

Which was good, she decided after a while, battling a crushing sense of letdown and thinking that her hopes that time would soften some of his anger might be to no avail.

Unless maybe she told him the whole truth about why she'd left him…

What would happen if she was open and honest with him about the past now? Would it help? Would he even believe her?

And what was her real motive?

That was the most important question.

Because if her motive was only to improve things between them—both to keep their history from negatively coloring his decision about Holt and in order to relieve some of her guilt—then maybe it was okay.

But if telling him the whole truth had anything to do with the other part of the cocktail swirling around in her? The part that had kept her awake last night pondering kissing him?

Then she should keep her mouth shut because she shouldn't do anything that might encourage her current attraction to him.

Better that he thought what he thought. Better that she live with the guilt and remorse and not risk her heart again.

She closed her eyes and shook her head, thinking how much easier it would have been if she'd come back to Merritt and found only nostalgia.

"Okay, I'm too hungry, and that smells too good."

That had been Marli's plan.

It was ten o'clock Tuesday night. The day of vets-helping-vets construction had begun at 7:00 a.m.

Dalton and all three of his brothers were among the crew and the work had gone on until seven o'clock that evening when everyone had left—except Dalton, who had stayed to help Marli clean up.

She appreciated the help, even though his attitude toward her hadn't improved—he continued to be distant, withdrawn and surly, speaking to her only when necessary, and even then without any warmth or friendliness or familiarity.

Still, Marli gave him enormous credit for coming at all and she appreciated that he'd facilitated the day's work, done a fair share of it himself and then stuck around to help her with the massive mess that was left behind. In gratitude, before beginning the cleanup, she'd offered to buy dinner.

Dalton had flatly declined and said he didn't want to waste the time to stop and eat, making it sound as if he was unwilling to spend one more minute than he had to with her.

So Marli had just gone on working, too.

But by the time they were nearing the end—and while he was taking yet another load of trash outside—she'd called what had once been his favorite local Italian restaurant and ordered what used to be Dalton's favorite sandwich—sausage, peppers, cheese and marinara on an Italian roll.

When he'd come in again, she'd informed him that

she'd ordered food for them both and left it at that. Now that the delivery had been made, the wonderful aroma that came with it seemed to be doing its job.

"I got a sausage sandwich for me and two for you," Marli said. "And there are pickles and chips and a big bottle of that sparkling lemon drink you liked."

"I'll take it."

Marli wasn't sure if that meant he intended to literally *take* his food home or not—which was obviously an option. But even if he refused to eat with her, she reminded herself that providing him with the meal was the least she could do. "Will you stay and eat it here or shall I just divvy it up so you can go home?"

"I'm too hungry to walk it across the street," he admitted. "Just let me wash my hands."

He held them up and it struck Marli that they, too, seemed bigger and more capable than they formerly were. They were fully a man's hands. And she couldn't stop the instant curiosity that came with the awareness about what they might feel like now— holding her hand, touching her skin...

She pushed the thoughts away and set the sack of food on the kitchen table, saying as she did, "Use the kitchen sink. There's paper towels to dry with." Then she went around the corner into the bathroom to do the same thing.

He was standing behind one of the chairs at the kitchen table when she returned. It struck her that, in days gone by, he wouldn't have felt the need to be so formal. Alone with her, he would have been right at home, taking a seat and doling out the food without hesitation. Now he was waiting for an invitation or permission. His posture was straight, his manner still businesslike and reserved despite the fact that they both showed signs of the long day's work.

"Sit down and relax," she suggested.

Not until then did he pull the chair out from the oval table and sit at the same time she did without seeming to relax one iota.

Marli emptied the food sack, which included napkins and plastic cutlery along with their dinner and the drink she'd ordered. As she passed Dalton his share, set the pickles and chips between them, and poured the bubbly, tart lemon libation into two of the glasses she'd taken from the cupboard, she just had to fill the silence.

"I can't believe everything that got done today— all the passageways and doorways widened, sturdy ramps at angles Holt will be able to manage alone. And that stair-lift? It looks great and now Holt and Bridget can sleep upstairs in a real bedroom. Plus with both bathrooms remodeled, he'll be able to use the toilet on his own, and that new shower upstairs makes it so he can handle his own shower without any help and come downstairs when he's dressed and ready. He'll be sooo happy about that."

"A seventeen-man crew can get a lot done in a day," Dalton said flatly, leaving more silence.

"I didn't expect you and your brothers to come, too," Marli went on. "An extra four men—that had to have helped. Especially with your suggestions. I didn't even know you had a degree in engineering. Those guys you were working with were all impressed with your suggestions for better ways to do things—I overheard a handful of them talking about how much more efficient your way made things and they said they'd have to remember it all for the next time."

She knew she was babbling, and she wasn't sure that was better than Dalton not saying anything at all as he seemed to pay attention only to his food. She decided to at least slow herself down and added a simple "Anyway…thank you again." It was a sentiment she'd expressed more than once to every man who had worked today.

Dalton only raised his chin to accept it.

Marli tasted her sandwich and judged it as good as she remembered. When she commented on it, Dalton made a sound that seemed to agree. But that was it and silence came again.

"So how did you end up majoring in engineering?" she said then, hoping maybe a direct question would work better.

Calmly and in no hurry, he used the napkin from his lap to dab away something she couldn't see from the corner of his mouth. "It just suited me more than the other options. I didn't want to choose anything the marines might decide to use that would put me behind a desk or in a room with a bunch of computers."

"Computers were definitely not what we needed today but the engineering came in handy," Marli mused. "Has it come in handy as a marine?"

"I haven't built any bridges, but seeing things with a problem-solving viewpoint can help in any number of circumstances—especially logistically. In Syria the site where the hostages were being held was well positioned, with some extra complications in the way of almost mazes within the building and in tunnels below it, giving the rebels an advantage. My reputation for dealing with unique logistical issues was why I was assigned the command."

"To figure out the best way in—like you did when I wanted to get into the abandoned gristmill to see if we could make the waterwheel go again."

Ohhh…that actually got a smile out of him. A tiny, tiny smile that came without him raising his gaze from his sandwich. "Yeah, like that."

Still, she ran with the memory. "Then I saw that window behind the bottom of the wheel—"

"And while I was figuring out an aboveground route, you climbed the wheel spokes to get down to the window and actually got in through it—"

"You didn't think I could. You were sure I'd slip

off one of the spokes and into the river, but then you did it, too—because it was quicker and more fun than your safer way."

Marli had been ten, Dalton had been eleven and by then they were heavily into having what she'd called their adventures.

"You couldn't get the wheel to turn again, though," Marli accused in the same teasing tone she would have adopted with him at that time.

"I hadn't been to the naval academy yet—get me in there now and I guarantee I'll make it go."

Marli smiled genuinely despite his emotionless expression. "I might still fit through the window but I know you wouldn't, so I'd have to get in and then open the door from inside so you could come in, too," she said. "It might be worth it—I'd still like to see the old thing turn."

"Or we could just use my original plan," he said as if they were actually plotting it.

But then, as if he'd just realized how much his guard had dropped, he resurrected it and went back to not talking and concentrating on his food.

It struck Marli that that was likely to keep happening if she didn't make more headway with him. And the only thing she could think to do was dive back into the past and correct the ideas he had.

Throughout the day she'd thought a lot about whether or not to be candid with him, always shying away from the idea of opening up too much of herself to him.

But there he was across the table from her and she'd seen that fleeting smile, she'd had just a crumb of reliving a better time with him, and suddenly it seemed like anything was worth getting back to that.

Only if your motives are pure, she cautioned herself, wary of the thoughts she'd had about him that were decidedly less than pure. But in this moment, reminiscing about their past, what she'd missed from him was the friendship they'd had as children. Surely that meant that she wasn't after any kind of romance. What she really wanted was just for them to be on a better footing so that they might get back to the innocent rapport they'd once shared.

Besides, she reasoned, at that moment they were both at their least attractive—they were grubby messes in soiled, raggedy old work clothes. She had no makeup on, her hair was in a now-stringy ponytail. He had sawdust in his hair and a smudge of dirt on the side of his face. This was the time to lay it all out.

Counting a whole lot on the power of the food and that hint of a smile, she took the leap. "Now that we both have cooler heads…could we talk more about when I left?"

"I don't know why we would," he said as if the subject had been talked to death and now bored him.

"Because you don't really have it right."

She waited for him to do what he'd done before and flare up. But apparently he really did have a cooler head now because that wasn't what he did. He opened his second sandwich, took a bite and remained poker-faced. Once he'd swallowed that bite, he said, "How do I not have it right?"

"I did have to run far and fast from you." She reiterated his words of Sunday night. "But not because I didn't have feelings for you…"

She hesitated, struggling with reluctance to bare her soul and the lack of practice she had doing it over the last seventeen years.

But this is your only hope of gaining ground with him…

Still, she couldn't quite do it head-on.

"You know how my mother programmed me," she said instead.

"Get out of Merritt, experience what the rest of the world had to offer, broaden your horizons, meet other people, or wither and die a slow, horrible small-town death," he recited.

"Yes," she confirmed. "And you know that I bought into it and was obsessed with getting out of here."

"I do," he said.

"But the thing is…" She hadn't said this even to him at the time. "When I found out there was going to be a baby and you were…"

The mere mention of what had gone on then

brought moisture to her eyes even now. She blinked it back, taking a chip, which she didn't eat, just to give herself a moment until she could go on.

"God, you were so good about it…" she said then. "I was such a panicked mess and you just…weren't. You took charge, you took care of me, even before that day I lost the baby, right from the minute I told you there *was* a baby, when you warned me not to say anything to anyone because you'd seen how your mother dragged Della Markham through the mud after her fake claim that Micah had gotten her pregnant. You said you would make sure your mother couldn't do the same thing to me. It was like you were stepping in front of a runaway train to keep me safe…" The awe she'd felt for that bravery was in her voice, awe she'd felt at the time but been too deep in her own turmoil to say.

She went on without encouragement. "I'll never forget how I felt when you said that you'd stand by me no matter how your mother or mine or anyone else reacted, no matter what they thought. That as long as we had each other we'd be fine. That you didn't need Annapolis or to be a marine. That we'd get married, have the baby… That it would just be a different kind of adventure and that nobody could do that the way we could… When you said that you'd still make sure we had a great life even if it didn't look the way we'd originally thought it would…" She took a drink of the lemon seltzer to wash down the lump in her throat. "It actually sounded good to me," she finished very quietly.

Dalton stopped eating, set both hands flat on the table, sat back and finally looked directly at her. But he didn't say anything. He just stared at her, studying her, waiting, maybe judging whether or not to believe her.

Which was how she knew she had to go on, no matter how hard it was to force the words out.

"I don't know…" she said. "Maybe even then something was telling me that Merritt wasn't as bad as my mother thought it was because I could actually see the two of us building a good life here. In a little apartment over one of the shops to start out. Getting married. Having that baby that would be the two of us…" Why did this put a knot in her stomach all these years later?

She took a breath and gave herself a minute, still suffering his silent scrutiny.

"Then all of a sudden there wasn't a baby anymore," she went on. "But the thing is…was…all that stuff you'd started me thinking about, that we'd been talking about, still didn't seem so bad…"

His eyebrows arched and she felt so much more exposed than she wanted to be.

But there was no going back now. "The thing is… was…" She couldn't bring herself to say it blatantly so she hid behind euphemisms. "There were *feelings*, Dalton…"

"You'd been telling me all along that those feelings were nothing but kid stuff. Puppy love," he challenged.

He was right—that was what she'd said every time he'd ventured into talking about what was between them. She'd had her mother's voice in her head, insisting that real, lasting love wasn't possible between two kids who didn't know what the real world outside Merritt was, who didn't know what real life was. Who *couldn't* know until they'd been beyond the stifling borders of their small town, before they were both grown up and had had experiences and a spectrum of people to broaden their horizons...

"Kid stuff. Puppy love..." she parroted. "I know that was what I always said. But when I did, you agreed with me," she reminded him.

"Well, we were just kids..." he hedged. "What did I know?"

"We knew what was going on around us—we'd talked about how we weren't like those other couples in high school who didn't want anything but each other. Who planned everything around how they could always be together. We both had bigger ideas—you never had a doubt that you wanted to go to the naval academy, that you wanted to be a marine. That was your number one priority—it wasn't me. At least it wasn't until the pregnancy..."

He conceded to that with a slight inclination of his head.

"Neither of us were ever all about romance. We more than liked each other but…" That had always been where those talks had landed—that they more than liked each other but it wasn't full-out love. It was puppy love. Kid stuff. She shrugged. "But then the pregnancy-test stick showed what neither of us wanted it to show and there were hormones and… regardless of what we'd called them, I had feelings. Enough to start thinking that even if there wasn't going to be a baby, I might want to stay together anyway."

She could see that her admission shocked Dalton. The truth had shocked her when she'd first realized it as well. And terrified her.

But she also saw something else in his expression that maybe followed the train of thought she'd followed years ago.

She went on. "I started to think, what if we stayed in Merritt, together? What if you gave up Annapolis and the marines and we just did that devoted-to-each-other couple thing? I made myself picture us… no college, working whatever jobs were open around here, having kids… My brother would go off to Annapolis and become a marine and then come back here to visit and rub your nose in it. Your brothers would go off to Annapolis and become marines and you'd hear about where they were, what they were doing—in places you'd imagined you'd be, doing what you'd imagined yourself doing. I didn't see you being happy stuck here in Merritt with me. I saw myself ending up like my mother…and you know where that led me—"

The smallest rise in his eyebrows granted the truth in what she was saying. "So you ran rather than talking to me?" This time it was a genuine question, not a contempt-filled accusation.

"Yes, I did. But it *wasn't* the cold, calculated decision you've been thinking it was. It wasn't because I *didn't* have feelings for you. It was because the feelings I did have kind of blindsided me and made me actually consider doing something I was sure we'd both live to regret. But I was so tempted… I knew if I saw you, if I talked to you, if we had that last summer together… I knew that even if I started to answer your emails, I wouldn't have been able to stop. The only way for us to go on to do what we'd both planned, what we both saw ourselves doing, was to—"

"Run and not look back," he finished for her.

"Make a clean, complete break and leave it at that," she reworded because all she'd done for so, so long afterward was look back. And miss him…

Until time—so much time—had helped her move on.

But she didn't tell him that. "I know if there had been a baby you would have come through exactly the way you promised. But once there wasn't a baby…" She wasn't sure how to say the rest. Choosing her words carefully, she said, "That miscarriage was really confusing for me. I was relieved. And so ashamed of myself for being relieved. And I was also so sad, too. When the baby was gone, there was a big part of me that didn't want it to be… But I knew there had to be some relief in it for you, too." She let that hang, waiting to see if he'd agree.

He didn't rush in, but after a long pause he said, "I get what you're saying, how messed up it was. We were just kids… I knew that. And yeah, I *was* relieved. But I saw what I felt about that as guilt instead of shame—although I'm not sure there's a difference. And at the same time…" He sighed, shrugged and shook his head in what seemed like bafflement. "Yeah, it was like I'd lost something I hadn't even had—it didn't make any sense to me."

"But you didn't still want to give up Annapolis, did you? You didn't want to give up becoming a marine and just stay in Merritt and marry me and work in the factory or at the lumber mill even when there wasn't going to be a baby anymore?"

He closed his eyes, his brows arched yet again and after another sigh, he opened those cobalt blues and said in what seemed like blatant honesty, "No. I mean, I thought about it, but… No, I didn't want to watch Quinn and Tanner follow Micah to the academy without me. No, I didn't want them to become marines without me. And your brother? To have had Holt go to the academy while I stayed here? To have him come back to lord it over me? No," he repeated unequivocally.

"Did you think about all that then?" Marli asked.

"I did," he answered honestly. "It all occurred to me before we lost the baby—what would have to go by the wayside, how things would probably play out down the road. But there wasn't any question about what I was going to do—we were going to have a *baby*. We were in it together. That's all there was to it. And then, when there wasn't a baby…" He paused again, then more quietly said, "I wasn't dreading the staying-together plan. There were things about that that I…liked. But when there wasn't a baby anymore, I didn't think there was any chance that you would even consider staying together—I thought I knew what you would say, that you'd be back on the bandwagon to get out of Merritt, and yeah, it felt like the right thing for me to be in line again for the academy, too. For the marines."

He shook his head, and in a voice that was suddenly raw, he added, "But doing what you did, the way you did it was…the worst. And you scared the living hell out of me on top of it. Whether it was for the best or not, it was…"

"I'm sorry," Marli apologized yet again. "It was just the only way I knew I *could* do it and actually go through with it."

That made Dalton frown, though Marli was unsure why. But after a moment he nodded. And in that simple, slow motion there seemed—finally—to be acceptance and full knowledge.

Enough for Marli to gamble a little more. "We *were* just kids, not ready to be parents, to settle down. We might have been able to make it work, but would it have been what was best for either of us?"

"No," he allowed.

"Instead we both ended up doing what we'd always planned to do, what we'd always wanted. What *was* best for us both. So the baby, the miscarriage, the way I left, all of that aside—us doing what we ended up doing was what needed to happen, don't you think?" she said, urging him to see that once and for all.

He took another moment, another breath. Then he said, "Yeah, I'd have to say that it was the best result for us both. It was just a damn rough detour to get there."

But at least now he understood why she'd done what she'd done, and maybe they could put it to rest, Marli thought.

Neither of them had eaten in quite a while and she'd lost her appetite for more food. Dalton must have, too, because he used the wrappers from his sandwiches to scoop up what remained and dispose of it in one of the empty sacks.

"It's late," he said in a weary but normal, not-contempt-filled, not angry or resentful voice. "Let's call it a night. I'll come back tomorrow to help you with the patching and detail work."

"You will?"

"I will," he said without any explanation.

"You don't have to…" Marli said, surprised that he was making the offer, and doubly surprised that it seemed to come as a neighborly gesture rather than some kind of duty.

But then he disabused her of that idea because he said, "I had checkpoints set up between here and Billings to verify that that was where Holt was really going this morning. I've had reports that he was where he said he'd be, and that he's in for the night. I'll be notified when he leaves for home and along the way again—"

"I didn't know you were having Holt watched."

"He isn't under round-the-clock guard—he's just being monitored there and back pretty much the way I'm monitoring him when he's here. Part of why I was sent was to make sure he doesn't go AWOL, remember? I'll be in charge of that again when he gets back, so I might as well do something constructive while I wait."

There still seemed to be a measure of rationalization in it all. Monitoring Holt's arrival didn't require him to be in the house and working in the meantime. But Marli didn't point that out as she cleared away the trash, telling herself not to look a gift horse in the mouth.

"That would be great," she said.

He headed for the front door and Marli followed him. She felt both physically and emotionally drained from the long day and the difficult conversation, and yet still, somehow, she wasn't looking forward to him leaving.

But that's what it was time for and she wasn't going to fight it.

She went out the door behind him, across the porch and into the yard, where he stopped to look up at the star-filled night sky.

So maybe she'd fight it just a little…

"I know you're successful," she said as his gaze came back to her. "Are you happy? Are you where you wanted to be in your life?"

He looked down at her and for the first time in seventeen years, it was the old Dalton she saw. Well, the old Dalton behind that finely aged face. "I am," he answered. "How about you?"

"I think I'm headed in the right direction."

He nodded thoughtfully.

"So…do you think we can be a little more okay now?" she asked tentatively.

"A little" was all he consented to. But he did it with just enough of an upturn of the corner of his mouth again to give her hope that she truly had put them on a better footing.

"I'll take it," she told him with a hint of victory.

He was looking closely at her again, this time

without animosity, just as if he was registering something about her. And even though she wished she was presenting a better view, there was something else in his eyes that distracted her from self-consciousness.

It was a warmth that turned her mind back to last night's thoughts about kissing...

Occasions when they had...

What it might be like now...

That particular thought brought her up so short that she actually drew back just a smidgen, warning herself that—of course—nothing anywhere near kissing was going on here.

But he *did* keep looking at her.

His eyes *were* delving into hers.

And he almost seemed poised for it...

Like in the old days...

It had to be her imagination, she told herself sternly.

But still she couldn't shake the sense that he was considering it.

It's just some kind of déjà vu...

Then his broad shoulders squared and he said, "I'll be up at zero five hundred. I can start work at zero five thirty."

That was what he was thinking about. Not kissing.

"*Five o'clock* in the morning?" she balked.

"If you leave a key for me to get in, I can go to work without you—since you're in the cottage it won't wake you up. All the sanding of the new wood can be finished by the time you get over here so you can prime and I can follow you with paint."

He'd thought this through…

While she had been thinking he might kiss her.

Wise up, Marli…

"If you're willing, I won't stop you."

Not a reference to kissing, she insisted to herself.

"Key on the top of the front door frame, like it used to be?" he asked, oblivious to the back-and-forth in her head.

"I'll make sure it's there again."

"See you when you roll out of bed, then," he said, the implication that she was a slacker actually touching on teasing.

"I'll try not to make it *too* late. But no promises," she countered, bantering the way she might have long ago.

He still stayed looking down at her. And she again couldn't keep kissing from coming to mind.

With some melancholy this time.

Then he said good-night and left.

She got the spare house key and went back out to leave it for him, spotting him just going into his own front door as she did.

He disappeared inside without so much as a glance back.

Not that there was any cause or reason for him to glance back. It was just something he would have done when they were teenagers.

But that wasn't where they were anymore.

They weren't in a place where good-night kisses happened.

They weren't where they wanted every last glimpse of each other.

And yet again, Marli felt her eyes well up with tears.

"You're losing it, Marli," she muttered to herself.

But as she put the key above the door and went inside for the night, she carried with her a mixed bag of emotions that she couldn't explain.

A mixed bag of emotions that had her wondering— just a little before she pushed the thought away—if it really was true that she was better off for her pre-dawn flee from him and the iron curtain of silence she'd dropped between them seventeen years ago…

Chapter Five

Dalton was awake at 4:00 a.m. on Wednesday, attempting to get more than the two hours of sleep he'd managed so far. Unfortunately, it just wasn't happening.

After last night's conversation with Marli, his head had been too full to shut down. It had continued churning for most of the night.

He didn't know why information coming this late was having such an impact on him. It didn't change anything. It was just a twist in a story that didn't matter anymore.

But it was one hell of a twist.

Never—not once—had what Marli told him even occurred to him. She was afraid she might *not* have wanted to leave town? She was afraid she might have wanted them to stay together? She'd had more than puppy-love feelings for him?

It was damn hard to reconcile that with the Marli he'd known. Her sights had been set on getting out of Merritt from the day they'd met…

He'd been walking home from Rusty Thorne's house at dusk one summer evening when he was nine years old, and from out of nowhere a voice had called, "Hey! Can you help me?"

Startled, he'd stopped, looked around in search of who had said it, but no one seemed to be there. He figured one of his brothers was hiding in the corn field trying to scare him and was about to move on when the voice called out again.

"I'm up here."

There was a huge oak tree growing not far off the roadside and it had taken him a minute to spot the person among the branches—it was that Abbott girl from across the street, Holt Abbott's little sister.

Dalton hadn't been sure what her name was. Holt had already developed his dislike of all Camdens the year before, but as for Holt's younger sister, Dalton had no reason to have contact with her or to have a second thought about her.

But there she'd been, up that tree, informing him that she was stuck without a trace of fear in her voice.

"You know that white cat with the brown ear who's always around?" she'd said. "He was up here, meowing like he was in trouble, so I climbed up to help him. I didn't think I was getting so high. When I reached for him he jumped down by himself. But now *I* can't get down. Could you tell my mom or my brother or something? Nobody knows I'm up here."

"My grandfather has a ladder… I could go get it…"

Which was what he'd done, dragging it for the two or so blocks from home to the tree and propping it as close to her as he could get it.

That was all the help she would take—when he'd started to climb up to rescue her she'd told him to just hold the ladder and she'd make it down herself.

It hadn't been pretty but she'd done it and when she'd gotten to him—rather than being scared or shaken or maybe crying the way he would have expected a girl to do—she'd been happy as a clam.

"You should have seen what I could see from up there!" she'd told him.

She'd insisted on carrying one end of the ladder to help him take it home, and talked his ear off along the way. She'd told him about the hawk she'd gotten a close view of as it flew by, the colors of the sunset that she'd watched and that there was a ginormous squirrel's nest in the top of that tree. She'd said that she was positive it held a whole family of squirrels so she was going to make sure to set a basket of nuts at the foot of it in the fall for them to stock up for winter.

She'd made him pause while she caught a small

frog in order to let it go later in the pond so it wouldn't
get out into the road and hit by a passing car. And
while she'd helped him rehang the ladder in the garage, she'd even brought up how much her brother
hated him and his family, informing him matter-of-
factly that she didn't blame Dalton for what grown-
ups had done and she didn't know why Holt did,
either.

Then, as she'd said her final thanks, she'd offered
payment for Dalton getting her out of the tree—she
would warn him about her brother's future pranks
and plots against him. She'd promised to do it at least
until she left Merritt—which she would do as soon
as possible because she couldn't wait to grow up
herself and get out into the world where she would
see and do *everything*—and when that happened,
Dalton would once again be on his own with Holt...

That had been his first encounter with Marli Abbott.

Dalton had thought she was kind of strange even
for a girl. He hadn't known quite what to make of her.
She wasn't a tomboy but she wasn't girly or giggly,
either. And she certainly wasn't shy. She was bold
and forthright and full of energy and pluck. And
something about her not being what he'd expected
had piqued his interest.

From that day on he'd been aware of her. In fact,
he couldn't have ignored her if he'd wanted to, because she'd seemed to count that initial encounter as

the beginning of a friendship. She'd had no hesitation in telling him she was going fishing after school—if he wanted to come. Or asking what he had planned and if she could do it, too. And she'd made good on her repayment promise by alerting him of any upcoming pranks from her brother. Once, when a particularly harsh prank had slipped past her and Dalton had been determined to retaliate, she'd given him a spider and revealed that Holt was afraid of them.

By the time Dalton was ten he was spending more time on the playground and after school with Marli than with anyone else. He'd even been willing to take the heat from his brothers for wanting to play with a girl instead of them.

Marli had just been more fun, more interesting. She'd always been up to something and he'd wanted to know what it was and to get in on it with her.

They'd gotten into scrapes. And messes. And trouble...

And here he was now, staring up at the ceiling enjoying those memories in a way he hadn't in seventeen years.

Leaving the way she had had turned everything upside down for him and soured even the best memories of adventures they'd shared.

He'd known she wanted out of Merritt worse than anyone he'd ever talked to. But never—ever—did he think she would leave him high and dry without a word. That was what he hadn't been able to comprehend. After what they'd been to each other since they were little kids? After telling each other everything, sharing everything, for her to do that? Nothing was more unlike the Marli he'd thought he knew. So he'd figured he'd never really known her.

But now this? Was it the missing piece of the puzzle that made the picture finally clear?

For her to have had any thought, any inclination at all to stay in Merritt and settle down was every bit as unimaginable as her leaving like she had. But if she'd genuinely had those thoughts, those inclinations, he knew it would have completely and totally thrown her for a loop.

He'd always believed that she had held tight to her mother's view that the feelings they'd had for each other at such a young age could only be puppy love.

Now she was claiming her feelings for him had been so strong she'd *wanted* to have that alternative life that the pregnancy had pushed them toward.

They *had* both granted that their relationship was special, even if they hadn't called it love. And, as with everything, they'd talked about it, made a plan to keep in touch through emails, letters, calls. To meet back in Merritt during vacations when she went away for college, too. After college, after he began to serve, they'd planned for Marli to come to wherever in the world he was sent or stationed to visit—something in line with her goals of seeing and doing and experiencing everything she could outside Merritt.

He'd been sure it would happen, that she would stick to the plan. He couldn't believe it when she'd cut him off cold.

But if what she'd said last night were true, he supposed it explained why she'd severed everything with him.

We can't go through our lives being the only people we've ever kissed, she'd reasoned pragmatically when they'd talked about the future. The couple thing was just a phase, yet another thing for them to explore the way they explored everything—together. Their friendship, she'd insisted, was forever. The couple thing was just living in the moment...

And he'd agreed. Although he would have agreed to anything if it meant he'd finally get to kiss her. He'd wanted to kiss her so badly he hadn't been able to stand it.

In all their rationalizations, he'd figured her feelings for him were the same as his for her—strong but without any decipherable category. She was just Marli, whom he wanted to go fishing with as much as he wanted to kiss. He hadn't looked beyond that.

If he had, what would he have seen? Would he have seen any indication that she was leaning in the direction of *wanting* the couple thing to last? To keep them together and in Merritt?

He thought back to his own feelings for her and

conceded that maybe they had been deeper than he'd admitted to himself. Why else would losing her have hit him harder than anything ever had before or since.

And if his feelings for her had been bigger than he'd realized, *was* it possible that Marli had had such strong feelings for him that she'd had to cut and run to be able to resist the pull of them?

Plus she *had* been pregnant—he thought that needed to be added in. And she'd just suffered a miscarriage, which had to have compounded and confused and also added to whatever she was feeling.

None of that had crossed his mind back then...

He made a wry-sounding, humorless laugh into the dark.

Maybe, when it came to emotions, they'd both been out of touch with what was really going on between them. Knowing how badly she'd wanted out of Merritt, Dalton realized her feelings for him must have been pretty strong for her to have thought for even a minute about staying. And yeah, it would have shaken the hell out of her...

Looking at her leaving from that angle changed things. It actually began to make sense out of her choices.

And now he was faced with a new question. What would have happened if Marli *hadn't* taken off? What if she'd told him she wanted to go through with the stay-together-in-Merritt plan?

Would he have done it? Even without a baby?

The answer was that he might have. Because he hadn't been devastated by the change of plans. He'd been okay with it. And she'd meant so much to him—he wouldn't have wanted to say no to her.

But what if that was how things had played out? Would they have been one of those high school relationships that worked, that lasted?

As he lay there and considered that, he couldn't say that he thought the odds were in their favor. Not when he'd wanted Annapolis and the marines as much as he had.

Not when Marli had been so driven to leave behind the small town her mother had convinced her would ultimately strangle her.

Not when they both really had just been kids with no idea how to build a good life for themselves. They likely always would have wondered what they'd missed out on. So no, he couldn't honestly say that he saw either of them being happy like that.

And if that was the case, then maybe she'd made the right call. He still couldn't approve of the way she'd taken off, shutting him out completely, but parting ways when there wasn't going to be a baby anymore really had been for the best.

It took a few minutes for that to sink in. But as it did, it let the air out of his long-held anger and resentment and outrage.

"Huh…" he muttered as this whole new standpoint took over.

But what did it mean for now?

It didn't actually *mean* anything, he reminded himself.

Their relationship was long, long over and done with. At this point, they were just two people who had come through it and out the other end to move on. Whatever feelings they'd had had faded and they really didn't know each other anymore.

Except maybe that wasn't entirely true, he thought as he raised his arms and clasped his hands behind his head.

I want to know how you are, who *you are now, what you've done, where you've been. I'm just curious about how life has worked out for you…*

That's what she'd said on Sunday night. It was classic Marli—inquisitive, nosy, interested in everything, determined to get to the bottom of everything, to know all the details…

That's what had gotten them into exploring every cave, every out-of-bounds part of the countryside— because she had to know *why* it was out-of-bounds.

That's what had sent them slinking into city hall's clock tower to see if there really were bats living up there.

That's what had sent them farther into an old mine shaft than they should have gone to see if the rumors about a hidden miner's skeleton were true.

That's what had caused them to sneak out late on a summer's night to see if ghosts haunted the abandoned lumber mill the way local myth contended.

That's what had caused them to steal a stick of dynamite from a construction site to light and throw into the lake to see what would happen.

That was what had led them to explore each other with just as much enthusiasm. Sex had been awkward and fumbling and *fun*, since Marli brought such joy and enthusiasm to everything she tried.

He did a mental spin away from thinking about that particular phase of the past. It just wasn't smart to dwell on it. Especially when last night, he'd found himself with a fleeting…

He didn't know what to call it…

A fleeting *something* that had had his hands itching to reach for her. His arms itching to wrap around her. His body itching to have her up against him.

So that was *not* where he would let his head go now. Or again.

But into the earlier memories? Into when they were companions, cohorts, conspirators?

If they were going to be around each other— and for a while they were—then maybe that part of what they'd shared wasn't such a bad thing to recall. Maybe it could actually allow a reset between them…

As he lay there he tried that idea on.

A reset might not put them back to being friends, but it at least might take them out of being enemies…

Since he'd arrived in Merritt, thinking about her, about the past, had been a bad distraction from what he was really supposed to focus on. It would be good to end that.

So let the water under the bridge be water under the bridge, he advised himself.

And for the first time he thought maybe he could.

Maybe he could even get another hour of shut-eye.

He closed his eyes to try.

Water under the bridge…

Understanding gave him closure.

It genuinely put an end to it all.

He knew it because there were no simmering ugly feelings inside him to deal with.

Everything was resolved and behind him and not going to get in his way anymore.

Except when it came to sleep—he still couldn't seem to get back to that.

Instead there was the image of Marli right there in his mind's eye again.

Looking the way she'd looked the night before, like someone who had put in a day of hard labor— and yet still so damn good…

Water under the bridge…

Everything resolved and behind him…

Good and bad over and done with…

History. Never to be again.

So why could he see himself clasping his hands around her upper arms?

Pulling her to him…

Slowly, slowly leaning in…

And kissing her…

Like he'd never kissed her before…

Marli was trying not to look. Not to stare. Not to ogle.

But there she was, acting as Dalton's assistant while he installed a new light fixture in the cottage bathroom, and she just couldn't stop herself.

It was late on Wednesday afternoon and between the two of them they'd made great progress on the finish work of the main house.

Along the way Dalton had noticed the box that contained a new light fixture propped near the back door—it had been delivered earlier in the day. He'd asked where she wanted it, assuming it was for the main house. When she'd explained that it was for the cottage bathroom, he'd offered to put it in for her and save her the cost of an electrician.

Actually, he'd insisted on putting it in for her.

He'd been as quiet today as he had yesterday but there was a big difference in his manner—the halo of ire that had surrounded him since that first day was gone.

She had to assume that what she'd told him the night before had caused the change. That maybe she had accomplished her goal and telling him the whole truth had put them on better footing.

She didn't address it, though. If her honesty had formed a scab over the old wound, she thought it better not to pick at it. But things between them were much improved, so when he'd insisted on putting in her light fixture, she hadn't argued.

Holt and Bridget had returned from Billings around four o'clock. There had been a few minor details left of the finish work but nothing she and Bridget couldn't do so she'd sent Dalton with her light fixture to the cottage. Just in case.

She'd hoped her brother might show him some gratitude—but she wasn't willing to test it. Not when another temper tantrum from Holt could rock the boat she'd worked so hard to steady with Dalton.

Dalton had gone out the back after a glimpse of Holt to confirm that he was home, and Marli had shown her brother and sister-in-law all the changes.

Bridget had cried openly, and even Holt had teared up. But when he'd said he didn't know how to begin to thank the vets-helping-vets group and Marli told him that he should start with Dalton— outlining the extras Dalton had done on top of facilitating the work of the other men—Holt had turned contentious again.

Marli had lost her patience, thrown up her hands at her brother, voiced her frustrations over his stubbornness and left him to his wife, fuming when she'd joined Dalton in the cottage.

"Everything okay?" he'd asked, obviously noticing her annoyance.

"Everything but Holt," she'd muttered, sighing before encouraging Dalton to start the light fixture project by asking what she could do to help.

Acting as his aid by handing him tools and electrical tape and caps *had* helped take her mind off her brother but it had put her focus on Dalton instead. That was where the looking, staring and ogling had come in.

It made her wonder if she'd have been better off leaving the rift between them. Now that it was lessened, she'd become all too aware of things other than his mood.

Things like how great his rear end looked in those worn-out jeans.

Things like how his back V'd up from a narrow waist into shoulders she never would have guessed could become so broad.

Things like the shape and pure bulk of the biceps he certainly hadn't had at eighteen, stretching the short sleeves of his plain white T-shirt to their limit.

Even things like the back of his neck were somehow more masculine than she'd ever noticed before. She'd never thought she'd fantasize about necks, but she couldn't stop imagining cupping her hand around his if he were to kiss her...

Luckily the light fixture took as little time to install as he'd said it would and by five the job was done.

But after thanking him once again for everything as he began packing his tools in his toolbox to leave, she realized that she wouldn't be seeing him until the next time he checked in on Holt. And for some reason, she didn't want that to be the case, so she said, "Since I got here the other day, I've only gone into town for necessities. I haven't had the chance to just walk Independence or go into the town square or check anything out… I'd like to do that—and buy you dinner to thank you for all you've done here. I know dinner is a small payment, but… Any chance?" She ventured the question tentatively.

He closed his toolbox and stood, holding it in the fist of one big hand beside his impressive right thigh.

"Okay," he said so easily it shocked her.

"Okay? Really?"

"Sure."

Oh, he was definitely different today.

"Can I have an hour to shower and change?" she asked as if that might be a deal breaker.

"I wouldn't want to go out until I have," he answered matter-of-factly.

"Then…say six? We can decide where to eat when we get there?"

"Okay."

"I can drive…"

"Okay."

He was letting her call the shots the way he had when they were young and she'd come up with an escapade. As they'd gotten older and their time together had turned into dates, he'd taken charge more, usually doing the driving and picking the venue. So this told her it wasn't a date.

Which of course it wasn't. And she didn't want it to be. Definitely not.

While she was sorting through that, he took his toolbox to the door.

"See you in an hour," he said simply.

"An hour…" she responded dimly.

But if he noticed how much trouble she was having acclimating to the alteration of things between them, he didn't show it. He just opened the door, went out and closed it behind him.

Leaving her to herself.

After a few minutes of watching the door as if he might come back through it to tell her he'd changed his mind, she forced herself to move.

She spent that hour showering, shampooing her hair, blow-drying it, and ultimately brushing it and leaving it to fall around her shoulders.

She applied a pale mauve eye shadow, some eyeliner and mascara—all with the intention of looking her best without seeming as if she'd put any effort into it.

She chose a flowered halter dress that she knew

accentuated her shoulders and might have been somewhat sexy and date appropriate, but reasoned that it was a cool summer dress for a warm summer night and nothing else.

Then she opted for a pair of strappy sandals.

And throughout the entire process she lectured herself mightily about her unwarranted and straying eyes, thoughts and emotions.

Dalton's improved spirits, his agreement to allow her to show her appreciation and to even spend a little time with her were exactly what she'd been aiming for. It amounted to a peace between them and that was it, nothing more or less.

She was lucky just to have reached an accord with him—that was enough of an achievement.

And if she cultivated it just a little, then maybe it could do her pigheaded brother some good. But even if it didn't, at least she'd know she'd removed the possibility of Dalton taking his anger toward her out on Holt.

Just keep everything in perspective, she warned herself as she added the final touch of a little lip gloss. She used the pockets hidden in the side seams of the dress's wide circle skirt to carry her keys, ID, credit card and lip gloss—for touch-ups—and headed for her car. Wondering as she did what had gotten into her to drift the way she had.

And determined that it wasn't going to happen again.

* * *

"I think I forgot how nice this town is. I've seen a lot of places but I have to say there's nothing quite like Merritt," Dalton said as he and Marli stepped onto the lush lawn of the town square.

It was nearly ten o'clock that night and they'd walked both sides of the main drag of the small town, pausing halfway for a dinner of grilled bratwurst smothered in sauerkraut and spicy mustard with side dishes of German potato salad and bowls of creamy white asparagus soup.

Finishing their stroll through town had helped work off the meal and build an appetite for dessert. They'd swung by Schnitzel Shack just as it was closing up and persuaded the owner, Larry Longaker, to make them one last dessert to go: a chocolate-hazelnut-filled puff pastry topped with a scoop of homemade ice cream and a smothering of hot fudge sauce. At their request, he'd cut it in half for them and put it in two paper bowls, all the while mock-scolding them for still being troublemakers who would keep him late. Then he had refused to let them pay for the treat.

They'd eaten it on their way to the square, passing mostly closed stores and businesses by then, and disposed of their empty bowls as they headed into the park that separated the business district from the residential section.

"I guess growing up here, we took how nice it is

for granted," Marli added as they passed a bronze statue. "But all these well-kept old houses, and Independence Street's quaint Victorian-slash-Old-West-style buildings, and the wrought iron street lamps and benches, and this…the square…it all makes for kind of a beautiful little town."

"And you'll have your office right in the heart of things."

She hadn't brought the key to it so they'd only been able to peer through the plate glass front window at the stack of paint cans she'd told him she was digging into tomorrow, but there was no denying that the location was prime. "I can't wait," she said. "As strange as that seems for the me-of-old. I've even joined the city council."

That made Dalton chuckle. "That *is* hard to believe of the you-of-old," he said. "I hope nobody lets a rat loose in the meeting hall."

It was a prank they'd pulled—and gotten away with undetected—as kids.

They'd been reminiscing about all the things they'd done as they walked and took in the sights, noting the changes and the things that hadn't changed. After getting into her car, as Marli backed out of her parking spot, Dalton pointed upward and said, "Remember when we got caught in the steeple that Fourth of July when you thought it would be the best place to watch fireworks?"

"But we didn't get caught until after the display

was over," she reminded him without remorse. "And I was right—we had a great view. It was worth having to wash all those stained glass windows by hand."

"It was," he agreed.

Their evening together had begun much like their day—with Dalton amiable enough but so quiet that most of the conversational burden was on Marli.

As the hours had progressed, he'd become less and less quiet until they were talking easily. Not quite with the same level of effortlessness or closeness as in years gone by, but at least like old acquaintances.

"And now home again..." Dalton said as she drove out of town the way they'd come in.

"When they start to roll up the streets, there are only a few other choices," Marli joked, hiding her reluctance to go. The same way she was hiding a lot tonight.

At the beginning of the evening, he'd been waiting at the end of the Camden drive when she'd backed out of hers. Dressed in a pair of jeans, a black long-sleeved Henley crewneck with the sleeves pushed up to his elbows, his hair clean and tousled just right, and his scruff trimmed to sexy perfection, one look at him had tested her vow to remember that this was not a date. As his attitude had slowly warmed up, it had become harder and harder to keep that vow in mind. There was no denying that—to her at least— the evening had felt increasingly date-like.

By now the change in the atmosphere between

them also wasn't helping. Dalton was more relaxed, his arm was across the back of her seat, his body angled just slightly toward her.

"How strange was it to run into Liz and Chuck?" Dalton commented then.

Liz and Chuck had been in Dalton's class. He and Chuck had been good friends so there were many double dates that had included Marli, Dalton, Liz and Chuck.

"We knew most of the people we ran into tonight," Marli pointed out. "What seemed strange to me was that neither of them have *ever* left. They got married the September after they graduated high school—"

"And are still married and have *five* kids—" Dalton said, marveling.

"And haven't even been out of Merritt on a vacation in all these years."

"At least not farther than the foothills where they have that cabin." Dalton did his part of the back-and-forth update they'd gotten. "You're right—if it wasn't strange running into them, you at least have to admit that it's strange that they've never set foot out of here."

"Even for their honeymoon." Marli did some marveling of her own at what they'd learned. "Didn't they always make it sound like they had plans sort of like we did? I mean, Chuck didn't want to go into the military but he applied to out-of-state colleges and Liz wanted to live with her aunt in Chicago and try acting or singing or something—"

"Do the math," Dalton encouraged. "Their oldest kid will be a senior in the fall."

"Ohhh…" Marli had only been thinking about there being *five* kids, not about the age of the oldest. "They were more like us than I thought." *Minus the miscarriage…*

"Uh, yeah. Apparently."

"They seem happy, though," Marli mused. "They laughed about being glued to Merritt so I guess it's been okay for them. It worked out."

"Yeah, it seems like it did," Dalton said with what almost sounded like some admiration.

For a brief moment silence fell, but just as Marli was putting them in the other couple's shoes Dalton altered course. "And Liz is Yancy Coltrain's sister…"

"And always has been," Marli said with a small laugh at the way that he said it as if it was new information.

"I think she's hoping you'll go out with him now that you're back."

Liz *had* hinted at that. "Small towns… I live here now and I'm single—I guess that makes me fresh game."

"For Yancy Coltrain…"

There was a tone in Dalton's voice that Marli didn't understand. But the thought of Yancy only caused her to shrug off whatever Dalton was getting at. "It doesn't matter if that's what Liz is after. Yancy is… Yancy. Holt's friend and no one who's ever done it for me. He's nice and I appreciate the way that he's loaned a hand with Holt, but—"

"So you wouldn't have gone to the ninth-grade dance with him?"

Marli had no idea what Dalton was talking about. "What?"

"When he and I were in ninth and you were in the eighth grade—remember you and I got into that beef over something?"

"Over you acting so goofy about the new biology teacher."

"Not only me. Me and every other guy in school and most of their fathers. And I wasn't acting goofy. I was just appreciating—"

"Her *biology*?"

"She had a *lot* of that…" he confirmed wryly. The teacher had also been a swimsuit model. Marli remembered that she had caused considerable uproar for her sole year teaching in Merritt. "I was just enjoying the view like everyone else—"

"I'd never seen you act like that—it was gross. And talk about strange…"

"I think it's called puberty," Dalton said as if it was a novelty.

"Yeah, I figured that out—in retrospect. At the time? Just strange."

"For me, too. I didn't know *how* to act. With Miss Ingalls or with you."

"You were acting the same as always with me," she replied because it was true. "Until after I told you I didn't want to hang around with anybody who was going all googly over a *teacher*, and that I wasn't going to keep waiting for you after school, just to watch you follow her like a puppy dog to do after-school jobs for her. I got fed up with how long it took for you to come find me when you were done."

"Uh-huh…" he said with an inflection that implied another *think about it*.

It didn't require much thought. "That was when things started to change with us," Marli said, recalling that time in their lives, their relationship. "We still went fishing and exploring and did all the same stuff we'd always done, but there was a difference. I remember that as the turning point because when you came around again you brought *flowers* and that was the weirdest thing *ever*. I wasn't sure what was up with that—"

"What was up with that was the first freshman dance that everybody was talking about."

"You'd said you didn't want to go to some *dance*, then all of a sudden you did—also weird. But when I told you you were being weird, you said we just needed to start doing those things like everyone else was. At fourteen that seemed reasonable to me. But

I still don't know where Yancy Coltrain plays into any of that."

"Yancy and I were in the locker room one day after baseball practice. This was back when you and I were on the outs, so I guess he thought that meant that I wouldn't be bothered by what he had to say. And he said a *lot*. He was all *googly* over you. He went on and on about how pretty you were, about your eyes and your hair, and he said he just needed— *needed*—to kiss you so he was going to ask you to the dance and try to get the chance."

Marli laughed. Then some other things from that time began to occur to her. "Didn't you give Yancy a black eye right about then? Wasn't that when he sort of joined forces with Holt in hating you?"

"Yep."

"You never would tell me what happened…"

"Nope," Dalton said with some humor. "Couldn't explain to you what I didn't understand myself."

"But now you do. So tell me," she challenged.

Dalton shrugged. "It was then, in the locker room, when he said that stuff about you. It wasn't bad, cocky, dirty stuff or anything, it really was just that he wanted to kiss you. But I couldn't stand the thought of that. Before I even knew what I was doing, I punched him—it was like a reflex—and told him to stay away from you. Quinn and Tanner were there and they started razzing me about why I'd care if you went to a dumb dance with Yancy. I said you were just a kid and he didn't get to go after you like that, but even then I knew that that wasn't really all there was to it. And it did get me to thinking about why it bothered me so much. I started to take a closer look at you even though you still weren't having anything to do with me. And when I saw you through Yancy Coltrain's eyes, I guess I finally realized you weren't all elbows and knees and braces anymore."

That might have been more flattering if Dalton hadn't delivered it as just another piece of nostalgia, something that could be admitted to now because it was irrelevant.

"Ah, puberty…" Marli said philosophically. "So that's why the flowers?"

"You bet. Picked out of Big Ben's garden right before it was going to be judged for the garden-show ribbons—I caught hell for that! And then felt like an idiot for bringing them to you when the whole hearts-and-flowers thing wasn't…us…"

"It definitely wasn't."

In thinking over the years on the progression of things between them, Marli had already identified when the subtle change had begun between them. She had recognized the flowers and Dalton asking her to the dance as the pivot point from "friends" to "something more." But from there the progression had been very slow. For a long while Dalton had just put effort into keeping them a twosome. He'd made sure to sit with her at lunch and on the bus; whenever there was a festival or a carnival or any town event, they went as a pair rather than as part of a group; and when it came to other boys he'd put himself between her and anyone who might even think about asking her out.

Eventually their relationship had evolved into the couple thing, but that hadn't actually happened until near the end of her sophomore year, his junior. It wasn't until his senior year that there was no disputing that they were *together.*

But thinking about it all now suddenly made her wonder about a few instances that might have been questionable. She decided to see what else she could get out of him that she didn't already know.

"What about the other times we had fights and went our separate ways for a while? There were a couple of girls you went sniffing after, but as soon as some other guy would start talking to me you'd show up again..."

"Pretty much the same thing—I might have had a bone to pick with you every now and then, but that didn't mean anybody else could have you," he confessed. But again, he said it so casually, making it clear that it had no relevance whatsoever now. Which of course it didn't.

So continuing in that casual vein she said, "Hmm... I don't know what I think about you getting in the way of me and other guys..."

"You have a second shot with Yancy..." he reminded her, calling her bluff as their respective houses came into view.

"Yancy's out but maybe you better give me a list of the other guys you got in my way with. There might be someone I'd actually want a second shot with," she said.

"Who can remember…" Dalton joked. Then, as she slowed and veered toward the Camden drive, he said, "Pull all the way back to your garage. I'll walk from there."

She made a wide turn to do that. If he was the one offering to make it more convenient for her, then there was no reason to give him special treatment.

Or at least that's what she told herself. It wasn't as if she was prolonging their evening by not merely dropping him at the end of the Camden drive the way she'd been about to.

He seemed to have moved on from their drive-home conversation, though, because as she parked at the entrance to the garage he said, "This was fun."

"It was," she said, turning off the engine.

"I'm glad we did it," he added.

"Me, too."

They got out at the same time and met at the rear of her car, where Dalton leaned against the trunk and placed his hands palms down on either side of his hips as if he were in no hurry to make that last walk home.

Marli was fine with that. She rested against the

car, too, separated from him by a respectable twelve or so inches, both of them looking out into the night as if there was anything to see but the dark stretch of her driveway to the road.

Then out of the blue Dalton said, "It makes a difference knowing what was going through your head when you bailed seventeen years ago."

That was apparent since he'd stopped being such a bear. But Marli didn't say that. She didn't say anything.

"I wish you had told me then," he went on, "but I get why you didn't—I know it would have freaked the hell out of you to have thought for even a second about staying here for any reason. And I don't know what I would have said if you'd told me you might have been into staying... It could have gone either way, for better or worse. And in the end, I know that we both did what we were supposed to do." He paused. Then he added, "So... I guess I'm done being pissed at you."

That was a relief. But all she said to it was a simple "I'm glad."

He shifted toward her just enough to face her and held out his hand to shake. "Let bygones be bygones?"

Not the same as being friends again. That made Marli a little sad. But still she wasn't going to turn it down.

She angled his way and took the hand he'd offered. "Bygones."

As kids they'd sometimes grasped hands like that when they'd made a pact, but always with only one rise up before a single definitive drop and release.

This time there wasn't anything but the clasp—her hand surrounded by his, which was now so much bigger, stronger and more calloused than she remembered.

She could have done a regular handshake or their old pact handshake and ended it when he didn't. But his grip was firm and warm and if felt too good so she just held tight herself as she looked up into his face.

It crossed her mind that Bridget should see him now. Her sister-in-law would be hard-pressed to find any hint of meanness there. Instead it was just a preposterously handsome face, wearing a calm, contemplative expression.

Those ultra-blue eyes of his were taking her in as if, for the first time since they'd reconnected, he could tolerate a close enough study of her to truly catalog how she looked now. It might have made her self-conscious except that there was something in those striking eyes that said he liked what he saw.

Then, in a quiet voice, he said, "After Yancy shot off his mouth in the locker room I didn't just realize you weren't all elbows and knees and braces anymore. I realized he was right—that you were the prettiest girl I'd ever seen, too. And that I liked looking at you—and being with you…for more than fishing. I realized that I liked looking at you even more than I liked looking at Miss Ingalls. And you were nothing then compared to now… How did that happen?"

He seemed to be thinking out loud rather than actually asking a question, so she just shook her head, unsure what to say, surprised by the compliment from him.

"From the minute I realized all that," he went on, "the thought of some other guy—any other guy— anywhere near you? Kissing you? That just wasn't going to fly…"

"*You* weren't kissing me then," she reminded him. "Not until a lot later."

"Not until March third, the year I was a sophomore and you were a freshman—but I was sure as hell thinking about it before that…"

Marli laughed a little again. "You remember the *date* of our first kiss?"

"You slipped on the ice walking from the yearbook-committee meeting we had after school, and I grabbed you to keep you from falling. I'd spent that whole meeting watching Roy McCauley trying to impress you and wanting to punch him, too. Then I had you there, I had a hold of your arm… I'd yanked you up against me just in reflex to keep you from falling…" He pulled her slightly closer with the hold he had on her hand now, the hold that was no longer handshake ready but was just keeping them connected. "And all of a sudden it was me who *needed* to kiss you…"

And she who had kissed him back—because it was something she'd wanted to do, too. For so long that it had felt overdue and she'd begun to wonder if he ever would…

Marli told herself to make a joke that would dissolve the charge in the air between them. But as she looked up at him, recalling the past even as she was, at the same time, solidly in the present, she realized that she wanted him to kiss her too much to do that.

Even when she reminded herself that this man held her brother's fate in his hands, that she'd just spent days working to untangle her history with Dalton so it wouldn't affect his decision and that a kiss now would only add a new complication, she still couldn't make herself do anything to prevent it.

Instead she felt her chin tip up just a fraction of an inch in welcome. Her lips parted ever so slightly in anticipation as he slowly came nearer…

And then he did kiss her and she couldn't have cared less about anything but that.

That kiss that had nothing familiar in it, that was all new…

That kiss that lacked all the tentativeness the boy had shown during their first kiss…

That kiss that was confident and firm and soft and gentle at once.

That kiss that was amazing enough to answer all the questions she'd had about what it would be like to kiss the grown-up Dalton. Yes, it was different, but it was also better…so much better…and every bit as impressive as the upgrade in his face and body…

So much so that she wasn't ready for it to end. When it did, she was a little dumbstruck and it took a minute before she was able to return to reality.

Keeping her eyes on him, she watched his eyebrows arch as if that kiss had taken him somewhere else, too, and he said, "Shouldn't do that… That's what got us into trouble before."

Nothing that good…she thought, comparing the long-ago kisses with that one.

But what she said was a reluctant, unconvincing "Yeah…"

Dalton was still holding her hand and he brought it all the way to his chest and tugged her along with it for a split second before he gave it back as if he didn't want to and took a step away.

Then he pointed a thumb in the direction of his house and said, "I'm gonna go."

Marli nodded while inside she had to fight to keep herself from stopping him.

"Night," he said almost inaudibly.

"Night," she answered.

He turned and walked down the driveway.

She stayed where she was, taking in every step and every detail of the view of him from behind. She had to laugh at herself a little, remembering how certain she'd been that at least now, because she was no longer a young, hormonal teenager, she wasn't at risk of losing her head after one glimpse of him, one reach of his hand for hers.

She definitely wasn't a young, hormonal teenager...

But the rest?

She wasn't at all safe from any of that.

Except that she had to be, she told herself.

There was too much at stake—not only for her, but for Holt and Bridget, too.

He said it himself, she thought. *We shouldn't have done that. It's what got us into trouble before.*

So they wouldn't do it again, she vowed. *She* wouldn't do it again or let it happen again.

No matter how much she was wishing right at that moment that it would...

Chapter Six

On Thursday, Marli left Bridget and Holt to complete the finishing work on the family home so that she could devote the day to painting her office. Not only was she in a hurry to get her practice up and running after eight months of living off her savings, but she also needed to be somewhere away from the Camden place and the chance that she might catch sight of Dalton. Somewhere where there wasn't the ever-present possibility that Dalton might come across the road.

Because from the minute her eyes had opened this morning, seeing him again had been what she wanted more than anything.

She'd thought that having him hate her and bear a grudge against her had been bad. But after the kiss last night, she was starting to wonder if she shouldn't have just left it at that.

For Holt's sake she'd done the right thing.

But for her own?

She felt as if she may have entered a danger zone.

Part of the problem was that she liked Dalton— plain and simple and underlying everything that had ever been between them. They'd always been kindred spirits. From the start of their friendship, she'd found it effortless to be with him, to talk to him. They'd always been companionable. Like-minded. They'd connected on a basic level.

She'd liked him as they'd grown from kids into teenagers. She'd liked him even when she'd been in love with him. And she liked him again now. Only now it seemed as if she might be coming to like him with some of that little extra oomph that had happened during puberty and that had eventually led to loving him. That was something that she couldn't let happen again—and the way she'd been feeling since last night had her more than a little worried.

Not that she had fallen instantly in love with him after that kiss. But since his contempt for her had gone away she had definitely begun liking him again. Maybe more than liking him again…

That had been in that kiss…

That's where the oomph had come from. That's where she'd entered the danger zone.

Wanting to see him, to be with him again the very

second she'd woken up this morning, was a part of that danger zone.

There wasn't anything in the future for them, she told herself as she locked the office's front door behind her and took out the tarps and rolls of tape for the pre-painting preparations. They had a past and that was it. Reminiscing, catching up, the nostalgia they'd enjoyed last night, had been fun but that was all a part of the past.

Kissing was...something else.

At least it was for her. She supposed it could have been just a revisit for Dalton, but it hadn't seemed like that. It had been such a great kiss...

Which made it all the worse. Too bad it hadn't gone the other way. If only she'd discovered he didn't kiss as well as she'd remembered. If that had been the case, then leaving her past feelings in the past would have been easy. Instead that kiss had knocked the stuffing out of her...

But they weren't the carefree kids they'd been on that March day when he'd kissed her the very first time. Carefree despite Holt's grudge against Dalton and the bad blood between their families because none of it had ever felt like it was truly connected to the two of them.

But now they were adults and adults just weren't free the way kids were. The issues with Holt were on a potentially disastrous field that was much bigger than his old pranks and revenge schemes had ever been, and she couldn't risk doing anything that might make that worse.

Not to mention, Marli now had a history of her own. A track record that gave her pause. Now she'd learned more about herself and what she was and wasn't cut out for. She knew more clearly the path she needed to follow and she couldn't afford detours that would just make more problems in her life. Not when she was fully aware of how what she said and did could negatively impact people she became involved with.

She and Dalton were good as friends—or maybe even just acquaintances who were possibly inching back to being friends. And she was fine with that, she told herself as she taped the trim and tarped everything she didn't want splattered with paint. They'd crashed and burned as a couple, the same way she'd crashed and burned with three other guys. So she certainly couldn't risk starting anything again with Dalton and messing it up a second time. It would mess too many things up. For Holt. For Dalton. For herself.

They weren't meant to be together. They weren't meant to be like Liz and Chuck or they would be where Liz and Chuck were now.

And that meant that she had to be on guard against wanting anything more from Dalton. Regardless of how difficult it was to ignore her attraction to him.

Regardless of how good it had felt when he'd kissed her a kiss that had been better than any she'd ever had.

But we weren't meant to be, she told herself firmly. She had to accept that, hang on to that, not forget that or lose sight of it for even a moment.

You can do it, you can resist the weakness you have for him and be strong, she assured herself. It was easier to believe that here in her office, where she was a professional and secure in the person she'd grown into and knew herself to be.

Then there was a knock on her office door.

She peered through the as-yet-uncurtained glass in the top half of the door to see that it was Dalton on the other side.

And with that single, solitary look at him, she felt every resolve, every vow, cave under the weight of pure joy that he was there.

Joy and the sudden awareness that she was dressed in tennis shoes with holes in them, grungy jeans, a faded red V-neck T-shirt with raggedy edges. Not to mention that she'd neglected makeup and pulled her hair into a stark ponytail—all with painting in mind, not socializing.

But not even the way she looked could persuade her to turn him away so she went to unlock and open the door.

"I'm not ready for business yet so I hope you haven't come for treatment," she greeted him.

"I did strain my shoulder a little this morning

moving some stuff for Big Ben but that's not why I'm here, no. I came to help you paint."

"Oh, you don't have to do that…you've done enough. More than enough…" That kiss was on her mind with the *more than enough*. Which only solidified that she shouldn't tempt fate by spending the rest of today with him.

"Actually…" he hedged. "I owe you an apology for the end of last night. I crossed a line—"

The kiss again—there was no doubt that's what he was talking about. "We both did," Marli admitted.

"It won't happen again," he pledged.

And once more she felt a wave of uncalled-for disappointment when she should have been one-hundred percent onboard with that.

"It's okay," she assured. "It happened, we're both to blame, it's over. You don't owe me anything."

"Then what if I just want to help you? I don't have anything else going on this afternoon and I'm not good with idle time. My grandfather isn't going anywhere today so he's on the lookout for AWOL attempts for me, and if we work together we can double the amount that gets done."

"What about your shoulder?"

"Minor. And it's my left not my right so I can still man a roller."

"I'm lousy with a paint roller. I do better with a brush," she said as more of her resolutions crumbled.

"Then we're the perfect team—I'll do the rolling,

you fill in with the brush, and I'll be on my best behavior. I promise—just friends."

As it should be. But also still disappointing…

"All right then, I'm not turning down free help," Marli finally conceded, stepping far enough out of the doorway for Dalton to come in.

He'd dressed for work, too, and yet he still looked great even in equally grungy jeans and a plain white crewneck T-shirt. Of course while her T-shirt was relatively loose, his fitted like a second skin, highlighting and defining the muscles underneath it.

But she didn't want anything about him or the situation to hold her attention like that so she tried to rein in any notice.

"Paint cans are still closed—you haven't started yet?" he observed.

"It's taken me until now to do the prep," she said. "I just figured I'd work into tonight."

"Nowhere for me to be tonight, either, and since Big Ben sees all, I think I can risk sticking around here."

And with that they got busy—painting, just painting.

There were the two separate exam rooms, the bathroom, the hallway and the outer office. It turned out that most of their time was spent separately as Dalton went ahead of Marli to roll the walls and ceilings and move on while she followed with the brushwork.

The process—and the fact that they turned on music they'd both shared a taste for—cut out most of the need for conversation. It really was just working together and it was nearly ten o'clock when they finished.

They stacked the empty paint cans just outside the back door that opened to a narrow alley, and left the tools soaking there, too. Marli would contend with them on another day.

While she relocked that rear door, Dalton washed his hands in the bathroom and then let Marli take her turn to do the same.

She found him on his cell phone when she came out, ordering pizza to be delivered to the office.

"I'm starving," he announced after craning out the front door to take note of the suite number of the office to give for delivery. "My treat tonight."

Marli tried to argue that she again owed him for his labor but he waved that away, said, "It's done, tip and all," and plopped down against the only surface that offered a backrest—the front of her tarped reception desk facing the door.

"Now tell me more about this acupuncture stuff while we wait," he decreed.

Since the walls were covered in wet paint and she'd yet to bring in any chairs there really was only one place to sit. So she had no choice but to join him on the floor, her back against the desk, too. But she made sure to keep as much space between them as she could.

"Acupuncture stuff…" she echoed. "I stick needles in people to make them feel better."

"Does it work?" he asked skeptically.

"How's your shoulder?"

"I'm feeling it," he understated his pain.

"Want to try what I'd do for it?" she asked.

"Needles…" he said unenthusiastically.

"No bigger than a hair's width. Is the big, bad marine afraid?"

"Where are you going to stick them?"

"In horrible places…" she threatened ominously. "Your hand, your forearm, your elbow—"

"Not my shoulder?" he said with increased skepticism.

"There, too, but not until after I cup that."

"Cup?"

"Kind of like a hickey," she said, the words slipping out before she could stop them. She knew she shouldn't have used that comparison or the hint of salaciousness that had tinged her voice but it was too late by the time she realized she had.

One corner of his mouth curved up wickedly. "You're going to suck on my shoulder?"

"What was that about best behavior?"

"You started it," he accused.

"I'm not going to suck on your shoulder," she said,

making sure to sound professional this time. "You'll just have to see what *cupping* is for yourself."

He pretended to consider it, then said, "Well, I don't suppose hairy needles and hickies can do much harm…"

Marli rolled her eyes at him and got up to go to one of the exam rooms. Luckily, she'd already brought some boxes of work things.

Bringing back the necessary equipment she kneeled down on his left side. "Push your sleeve up above your shoulder as far as it will go," she instructed.

She hadn't anticipated the impact of seeing his biceps bare. The sight made her mouth go dry.

Or maybe that was just thirst from not enough fluids while they'd worked. Yes, surely that was it.

But the view of taut skin over bulging muscle made that excuse difficult to believe.

She positioned the first suction cup on the front of his also-extremely-impressive shoulder, attached the pump and vented some of the newly inspired energy into its pistol grip to pull the air out of the cup until it adhered and drew a mound of his skin up into it.

"I want this tight but not painful…"

"Feels like I could pop it off so maybe a little tighter."

She gave the pump a few more squeezes and stopped, going on to add three more cups on the outside, the back and the top of his shoulder before she inserted the needles in spots she'd purposely left between the cups, along with some on his arm and hand.

"Huh… I saw those go in but I didn't feel anything," he said when she'd completed the task.

"Now we just let it all do its job."

"And you think this will do something?"

She gave him a wait-and-see shrug and sat back against the desk again.

"You do this to your brother—along with real medicine?" he asked then.

"Chinese medicine is *real* medicine. It's been around even longer than western medicine," she defended. "I give herbs the way MDs give prescriptions. And even when western medicine is being used, acupuncture can be a good add-on."

"But what can it do to counteract what your brother's gone through? Do you think you can return the use of his legs?"

"Like I said, what I do can be a good add-on to the treatment that Holt has gotten so far. No, I can't return the use of his legs. But acupuncture can speed healing, balance his system, boost his strength and resilience and energy, and help with emotional adjustments to the changes he's dealing with, too, by calming him down when he gets stressed. The body and the mind have strong self-healing abilities and acupuncture can encourage those abilities."

"Uh-huh…" Dalton said, still clearly unconvinced.

"And regular doctors at V.A. hospitals let you do this?"

"Some more willingly than others and only when they're sure it won't interfere with what they're doing, but yes. And even doubters like you have admitted that Holt has done better, quicker, than a lot of people with injuries like his—although still they haven't jumped on any bandwagon, they've just *allowed* that he's been kind of remarkable here and there."

"But you take credit?" Dalton said with an amused smile.

"I take some of it, yes," Marli said proudly.

Dalton grinned. "That's my girl," he said approvingly.

When they'd been friends, that kind of positive reinforcement from him was nice to have. But seeing that grin and the sexy lines it put at the corners of his gloriously blue eyes also made her think *god he's gorgeous.*

And that got her thinking about kissing him again...

He drew her out of that contemplation by saying, "Well, I'll admit that my shoulder is loosening up— who knew hickies could help something."

"If you can eat pizza one-handed I'd like to leave it going for a while."

"I think I can manage. Where did you go to school for this?"

"New York and China."

"You went to *school* in China?"

"For six months my last year of acupuncture school. It was a special, select program and I had to apply a bunch of times—"

"But you weren't going to give up trying."

"Because I really wanted the experience. And I finally got in."

He nodded, "Sure," he said as if he would expect nothing less.

But that, too, was said with a tinge of admiration which reminded her that he'd always been her strongest supporter, her greatest cheerleader, and again it was nice to hear. That *hadn't* always been the case with other people in her life. Her tenacity had irked some friends and male partners who had called her a *dog with a bone* in irritation.

The pizza delivery boy appeared at the office door. Marli got up to get it and after thanking the teenager she brought everything back. Dalton's legs were extended straight out in front of him, crossed at the ankles, and she set their delivery on the floor alongside them. Then she sat down again, facing him over the pizza box.

"I got the works," he said as she pulled up the lid to the box. "Sausage, pepperoni, meatballs, peppers, olives, mushrooms, extra cheese and extra sauce— same as always so I guess I hope your tastes haven't changed."

"On thin crust," she added, realizing how hungry she was as the smell wafted to her. "Perfect."

There were also two waters, paper plates, napkins, two sets of plasticware and a handful of peppermints. "They said it was too late for salads," he told her. "I don't know why, but after nine they only do pizzas."

"Good enough," Marli said as she put a slice of pizza on one of the plates for him and handed it to him.

He set the plate on those impressive thighs as she took a plate for herself and a slice of pizza that went to her mouth for a bite.

"Mmm, either that's the best pizza in the whole wide world or I'm starving, too," she said.

"Tastes pretty good to me," he judged.

As they settled into eating, he picked their earlier conversation back up. "Where else have you been besides China? What have you seen? Where have you lived? Worked?"

"I've been to a lot of places. Besides China, I've visited Japan, most of Europe. I did one trip to South America. I spent a month in Namibia and Cape Town—Namibia is where one of my fiancés was born. I went to Israel, spent a week in Prague, a couple places in Canada, some resorts and ruins in Mexico. I visited Vietnam. And the States—Hawaii, of course—and I've seen all the big sights in the US, I went to Alaska—"

"I thought I'd been to a lot of places, but I think

you've topped me," Dalton said with a laugh. "I haven't seen all the sights in the US and I haven't been to Alaska."

"As for where I've lived and worked, that would be Los Angeles for the last year of high school and then four more years for college. After college I went to New York for acupuncture school and to work for two years after that. Then I moved to Denver and was there until eight months ago."

"When you decided to come back to Merritt," he said, still sounding as if he couldn't quite believe it. He took another piece of pizza. "You never did fail to surprise me."

"Merritt still feels like home—well, actually I didn't start to think that until the second year in L.A."

"Not the first?"

"The first year was kind of a blur..." She'd been so miserable over him that it had been nothing but tears and moping. But what she said was, "I didn't socialize or make any friends my senior year of high school, I just kept to myself. I did what I needed to do to graduate and that was it—I had a lot to get over..." Which was as much as she was going to admit to. "When I started at UCLA, though, I thought I should put some effort into my new life and I had some rude awakenings—that was when Merritt itself and life here initially began to appeal to me, to *my* surprise."

"What kind of rude awakenings did you have?"

"Oh, a lot of things. I didn't fit in, the people I met were different than I was used to—some of them were more sophisticated, some of them were just more street-smart, some of them had their own agendas that I didn't see coming. I guess I was too trusting, and without any backup or safety net—" Without him… "I was a little like a lamb to the slaughter at first. Guys with way more experience and way more game started coming after me—"

"Because you look like you do," he interjected as a simple statement of fact.

"I'm not sure about that. I think what I looked like was just a country bumpkin—an easy target. As soon as the guys who were coming around found out that I liked to explore, I ended up in spots I didn't want to be in—"

"Spots…" Dalton repeated, sounding concerned and protective. That tone used to mean that anyone who harmed her would have him to answer to. "Did bad things happen to you?"

"No, but there were some times when things could have gone really badly. It was pure luck that they didn't. When taking me to *explore* a great area of woods meant getting me in the middle of nowhere for no reason but to—"

"Jump you?"

"Sort of. But when I said no he left me there and I had to get myself back to civilization. Fortunately a car full of girls my age stopped while I was walking along the side of the road and offered me a ride. Another time a get-together I was told was *just the kind of party that happened in L.A.* turned out to be an underground rave full of hardcore drugs and..." She grimaced, "And kind of rampant group sex. I had to get out of there on my own, too—in a hurry. There was just a lot of out-of-my-league things before I learned to be more careful. More guarded, less gullible. You know, Merritt has had some bad apples but on the whole most people look out for each other. I had to learn to look out for myself." Because she didn't have Dalton always at the ready to do it for her anymore. "When I pieced that out it made me homesick for Merritt." And for him all over again. "Not homesick enough to come back then and hide out, but still, that's when I started to think that coming home to Merritt someday might not be so bad after all."

"But you *didn't* come back. You pushed through."

"So I *could* see and do everything, go everywhere I wanted, just with my eyes more wide open."

"Only to end up here anyway."

"But *after* I've been a lot of other places and met a lot of other people and done a lot of things," she reminded. "Now it's a choice."

"Have you come back to hide out?" he asked, taking his third piece of pizza.

She laughed. "Now I've had seventeen years of taking care of myself and I'm told that I might be *too* good at it, so no, I don't need to hide out from anything. I'm just older and wiser and I realized that this is where I want to be."

She used a plastic knife from one of the sealed cutlery sets to cut one of the pieces of pizza in half.

"Who told you you were too good at taking care of yourself?" Dalton asked then.

"My last fiancé. And his girlfriend-slash-my-best-friend-and-office-mate."

He helped himself to yet another slice, too, frowning so much it made his eyes squint. "That sounds like a tangled web...but it does bring me to my next question. Your *three* engagements—tell me about those."

Marli made another face to show her reluctance.

"Come on—think of it as payment for my painting today," he cajoled.

"That might be too high a price."

"Sorry, you should have negotiated before, now it's the bill you're stuck with," he said.

This was the way things between them had been when they were younger—talking freely with each other, joking and teasing, with no judgement. It was part of what had made her like him in the first place. And it made it seem as if there was no reason not to be honest even on this particular subject. So she was.

"Well, there was Nolan—the guy born in Namibia. I met him right after I started acupuncture school and ten months later he proposed—that was why we went to Namibia, so he could introduce me to his grandmother and show me where he'd grown up. Then there was Clint—he was a Denver physical therapist I met at a seminar. We went out a year before we got engaged. Then there was Arnie—he did my taxes—"

"Among other things—like your best friend who was also your office mate?"

Marli made another face. "Yes."

"Still, not really getting much information in all that... Who dumped who along the way?"

"I ended the first two and was literally within minutes of ending the third when Arnie—and Alice—did it for me."

"I need more details," Dalton demanded after offering her the last piece of pizza and taking it for himself when she turned it down. "Why didn't you make it to the altar *three* times?"

Marli shrugged. "I'm trying to figure that out. Maybe marriage is a bad fit for me? Maybe I'm just not the marrying kind. As it gets close, I always find that I just can't do it."

"But you keep accepting proposals?" Dalton said as if that didn't track. "Why would you do that if you're anti-marriage?"

"I'm not *anti*-marriage," she insisted. "I mean, I don't want to go through my life alone, end up alone. I do want a family. It's just that when the engagements are really cemented and the *we's* start—"

Dalton laughed. "What the hell are the *we's*?"

"The *we's*—*we* have to do this, *we* have do that,

we can't do this or that, *we* might need to move for his job or his family—"

"Are you saying you only want things your way? On your terms? Because that doesn't sound like you—you were always up for my ideas as much as I was willing to go along with yours."

"It's not that I only want things my way, no. But when the *we's* start coming they bring *we can't rock the boat. We need to keep a lower profile, mind our own business, not get involved in things that don't directly concern us.* And then it gets to *when you're my wife I need you not to be so outspoken so you don't make me look bad. When Aunt Jenny screams at the waitress don't step in, we're all going to be part of the same family and you just have to roll with those things. Don't give your opinion so much. It's not your place to interfere and you embarrass me when you do that*—"

"Did this happen with all three of these guys?"

"All three. It came with the rings. Once it became official that we were a unit, it seemed to sink in for all of them that whatever I did or said could reflect badly on them, or cause more upheaval than they wanted. For instance with Clint I climbed over his neighbor's fence to give the dog water on a blisteringly hot day when the neighbor didn't leave any, and Clint had a fit because the neighbor was temperamental and got mad. Clint liked to stay *under the radar*, he said he didn't want to be dragged into my *causes,* he didn't want me making enemies that he had to deal with—which makes some sense…"

Dalton smiled. "Did you tell him he should be grateful that you didn't kidnap the dog?"

He knew full well that she'd done exactly that when she was thirteen, kidnapping the overbred dog of a family she babysat for. "I just took her home with me one day and kept her until it was too late to breed her through that one heat so she could have a rest. And you helped—you checked on her that day when I couldn't get there—"

"Which you didn't rat me out for when they caught you, so thanks for that," he said with more humor.

"But anyway, that was my problem when the *we's* started. Behavior they hadn't minded in their girl-friend turned into a problem once I was their fiancée and I wasn't alone in the accountability. It becomes an issue."

"I think that might depend on the man," Dalton suggested.

"I don't know… I can't deny that sometimes they had a point—I nearly lost Arnie his job—"

"Arnie was fiancé-number…"

"Three."

"The taxman who did your best friend and of-ficemate?"

"Yes. But before that, there was the time when I needed to pick him up after work. While I was wait-ing for him to come out there was a couple in a truck nearby, fighting, and the guy punched the girl in the face. I got out and yelled, *Hey!* The girl nearly fell out of the truck to get away from the guy but he was coming after her again, fists clenched. I ran over to her, screaming that I'd called the police—which I had—and the guy got back in his truck and tore out of the parking lot."

"And that was bad why?"

"The guy was the son of Arnie's boss. It got messy, there were assault charges brought against him, I was the witness and Arnie's boss was supremely ticked-off. He threatened to fire Arnie, and even though he didn't end up doing it, Arnie was told I was not welcome anywhere near the office or at any events the company might ever have—like the big Christmas bash they threw every year. Arnie was sure I'd ruined his chances for ever being promoted."

Dalton's eyebrows arched at that. "Yeah, that sounds like a bad situation all the way around. Still… I can't fault you for what you did. This stuff just seems like you being you. It's not your fault that the boss's son was an abusive jerk. If he didn't want to be faced with assault charges then he shouldn't have assaulted anyone."

"Well, the boss didn't see it that way. His son wasn't the problem, I was. And by association, that meant Arnie was, too. When the *we's* start, me being me seems to stop being okay because I'm not the only one bearing the brunt of the fallout. And that's when I start to hear my mother's voice in my head, talking about the sacrifices marriage takes, about the need for endless compromise—the things she saw as ruining her life. And I can see that there have to be sacrifices and compromises, I understand that, but I'm just not sure I can *do* it. Especially when I remember how rotten my mother felt in her own marriage about the sacrifices and compromises she had to make."

"If you felt like that the first time you got engaged, how'd you get into it two more times?"

"All three times, the shift in attitude didn't happen until we *were* engaged. So at the point of the proposals, I thought that I was in better relationships than the one—or two—that had come before. I thought that maybe Clint—and then Arnie…were… you know, okay with me being me."

That came out haltingly because with each relationship it had seemed as if—when they'd said they loved her, when they'd proposed—they didn't have a problem with her, that they'd accepted her, liked who she was—and it had come as somewhat of a jolt when that hadn't been the case. All three times. "I think it's really your fault," she added.

"My fault?" Dalton exclaimed.

"Well, you knew me—the best and the worst of me—and it never rattled you. It didn't seem outside the realm of possibility that I'd find someone else who—like you—didn't have issues with the way I am."

"Are you saying no one could live up to me?" he joked.

She rolled her eyes at him but refused to give him the satisfaction of confirming it.

Her silence seemed to serve as confirmation enough, though, because he smiled a smug smile before he returned to what she'd said earlier, "So you were literally within minutes of ending the third engagement when…what? The guy and your best friend pulled the rug out from under you?"

"I actually had plans to end things with Arnie over dinner—it was supposed to be just the two of us, the ring was back in the box and in my pocket, ready to be returned. Then he showed up with Alice—she is a masseuse, she answered an ad I put out for someone to share my office. For five years, we were in the office together almost every day, and we'd become friends. Close enough for her to hang out with us both sometimes. But it turned out that there was more than that going on—they'd been seeing each other behind my back for about three months and *he* wanted out of the engagement to be with her. And if that wasn't enough, Arnie wanted to tell me why he preferred Alice and how flawed I am, and Alice—who I thought was my friend—also wanted to chime in—"

"They ganged up on you? That stinks!"

"It really did," Marli confirmed, feeling a fresh pang of the pain and humiliation she'd experienced when it had happened. "Between the two of them, they'd decided that—besides me being a troublemaking buttinsky—my relationships didn't work because I'm *too* independent, *too* self-reliant. They said I'd made them both feel unnecessary and unimportant. Arnie said he'd never thought I was all-in with him, that he felt *expendable*—"

"That's quite a pile-on… But it sounds to me like they were justifying their own dirty deeds," Dalton observed.

"They said they were trying to help me—like an intervention—so I could change and have better luck in my future relationships."

"Oh, geez…" Dalton responded in disgust.

"Yeah, wasn't that sweet of them…as if the whole thing was somehow okay if they pretended they were doing it for *my benefit*," she said quietly. "I mean, I was glad to be out of the engagement with Arnie, but I didn't really need all that—"

"It was lousy all the way around," Dalton concluded. "It's one thing to call off an engagement, but to flaunt their screwing around and act like you had it coming for *any* reason? That's low."

She'd thought so. And it had knocked her for a loop.

But it was over and she was determined to salvage what she could out of it. "Still, after three strikes, I decided I need to take it as a sign. Not everyone is cut out for marriage. Maybe I'm one of the ones who isn't," she summed up as she gathered the trash and then turned to the red-and-white-striped peppermints. They each took one.

Dalton turned contemplative. "It's funny—when we were kids I always thought you were fearless. But it's kind of the opposite, isn't it? You were actually over-the-top afraid of getting stuck in Merritt seventeen years ago, and since then you've apparently become over-the-top afraid of marriage, too. So far over the top that I think you might actually have some phobias."

"I don't know that I'd go that far," she contended. "When it came to Merritt, I just wanted to see other places, meet new people, experience more than I ever could have here—"

"I know that's what you always said, and back then, I believed that that was all there was to it. But I don't think that alone would have made you panic the way you did at just *considering* sticking around even after there wasn't going to be a baby. It's good that you worked through it. Maybe you'll be able to work through the marriage-phobia if you put your mind to it, too."

"Or maybe I'm not marriage-phobic, maybe I'm just not cut out for marriage. You're not married— does that make you marriage-phobic?"

"I only almost got there once—not *three* times," he reminded her. "And I ended it because I thought better of it, not because I felt like I was about to be swallowed up by quicksand."

He'd almost gotten married once? That was news to her. He'd only said before that he wasn't married and never had been. He'd omitted any mention of a close call. And it wasn't news that sat all that well with her...

But they weren't talking about that. He went on without leaving her an opening to dig into it.

"You run because you're so scared of the stuff your mother felt about being married," he theorized. "The same way you ran from Merritt before it could get a hold on you because your mother had made you feel like it would ruin your life."

"You're forgetting that there's also the issue of me being me. It's when that stuff starts that I see that it isn't going to work. It's one thing to get myself into things, it's something else when what I do or say drags someone else into trouble they can't handle. If I'm single there's no worry about that—that's not a phobia, it's just common sense."

"Again, I think that's on the men you've met. Phobic or not, afraid or not, you're strong, Marli, you've always been strong. It's what makes you go to bat for complete strangers when you see a need for it. I think you've just hooked up with men who aren't as strong. When we hung out I knew what you could get us into and it didn't bother me," he pointed out. "I'm just saying that your mother hated Merritt and blamed it for a lot, but you worked through that to see the truth for yourself. Now maybe you're marriage-phobic because of that same thing with her and maybe you're letting that have more sway than you should."

Dalton had known her well way back when. In the old days she'd been inclined to give a lot of weight to his opinion, to consider his viewpoint. Should she now?

She wasn't sure.

But it seemed to her like they'd gotten into enough about her failures for one night so she skirted any more discussion on the subject by saying, "I should get those cups off and the needles out."

He nodded as if he knew she'd reached her limit on the conversation. Rather than push her any more, he said, "I'll be glad to have my arm back."

She scooted closer so she could reach him. "Ordinarily I would follow this with a little massage of the area but it's up to you…" she said tentatively in case he didn't want her to. For her own part, she was unsure if she should.

"Okay," he consented as if he wasn't worried that it might have any non-therapeutic repercussions.

Which, of course, it wouldn't have because she *was* a professional, she reminded herself.

"I'll be right back," she said as she gathered her instruments, taking them back into the exam room. She left the cups to be cleaned later, disposed of the needles in her hazards box, and put a few drops of analgesic oil into her palm.

Then she returned to the front office, knelt down beside Dalton again, shored up her defenses and tried very, very hard to actually *be* completely professional as she placed her hands over his shoulder and began her massage.

She'd done this to any number of people, any number of times, on any number of sizes and shapes of body. Not once had it ever had any effect on her aside from satisfaction at helping her patients. It was just part of her job.

So why was she feeling so much now that wasn't in any way professional?

Yes, he had a uniquely large, sleek-skinned shoulder. Yes, he had astonishingly well-honed biceps and a back that was more powerfully-muscled than most. But she'd treated other well-built men before. She should have been impervious.

And yet the instant her palms covered his warm skin she couldn't stop being ultra-aware of every detail. The contact felt supercharged and sensual, and she couldn't downgrade it to simply professional no matter how hard she tried.

And she did try. With everything in her.

But nothing worked to block those thoughts of the end of Wednesday night and his kiss, which only made touching him more complicated for her.

Dalton wasn't saying anything, he wasn't moving

into or out of the caress of her hands, of her fingers compressing his muscles. He wasn't saying it felt good or that it was helping or hurting or anything. He was just sitting there, face forward, letting her do her job.

Her job. That's all this was—her job. And she wouldn't let any inconvenient attraction keep her from doing it to the best of her ability.

Until she began to wonder if she'd been doing it longer than she might have on anyone else…

The oil had absorbed into both his skin and her palms, so possibly…

Yet there she was still doing it.

Be stronger…

You were going to resist this…him…

So do it!

Summoning controls that were nearly out of reach she finally drew the massage to a conclusion, sitting back on her heels to put some distance between them. Not much, but some.

"Any better?" she asked, meaning for her voice to sound calm and unconcerned, the way it would have been had she been addressing any other client. But the feebleness in it gave her away.

His eyebrows arched high and he closed his eyes. He seemed to be holding his breath and she wondered suddenly if she'd done something to hurt him.

"Sometimes with this kind of treatment it can feel a little worse before it gets better," she informed.

"Not worse…" he said gruffly.

He opened his eyes, rolled his shirtsleeve down and pivoted just slightly toward her. And when she looked into those now-open blue eyes, she became aware of the raw effects that her touching him had had on him, too.

And that, for some reason, caused her own defenses to drop away. When he raised his left hand to the side of her neck, when he leaned toward her enough to close the distance she'd put between them, when he kept his eyes locked on hers as he moved nearer and nearer until he was kissing her again, there wasn't an ounce of resistance in her.

Instead she leaned into it, parted her lips in answer to his, raised a palm to his chest, and let that kiss have her without another thought of anything but how much she'd wanted it to happen again since the minute he'd stopped kissing her the night before.

From the time she'd gone into the cottage last night until right then she'd half-wondered if that kiss could really have been as good as she'd thought it was. But this one not only confirmed her opinion, it improved upon it when his mouth opened a bit wider and his tongue came to reintroduce itself.

Her hand drifted up to his side and his went from her neck to the back of her head. With that, he braced her in place so that he could deepen that kiss that she was responding to in ways even she hadn't known were possible.

His right arm came around her, pulling her to sit rather than kneel beside him, to bring her far enough in to almost—but not quite—meet front-to-front.

They went on kissing and kissing and kissing without restraint, with more and more zeal, more vigorous tongue-play, until Marli lost all track of time. She couldn't think of anything *but* kissing him and the fledgling ache for more than kissing…

But just about the time she began to recognize that, Dalton showed once again that he had more wherewithal than she did and gradually reversed things, pulling out of that kiss to drop his forehead to her hairline with a sigh. "I wasn't going to do that again…" he said in a whisper.

"Me neither," she whispered back.

But they stayed the way they were, head-to-head, both of her hands on his chest now, his hand behind her head and his arm around her also keeping them together.

They sat there that way for too long for it not to be clear that there was no eagerness on either side for them to separate.

But this time it was Marli who finally found her resolve, taking her hands off him, straightening up. Although not too far too fast because he didn't let go for another moment.

Then he did, sitting against the desk again, showing his palms as if in surrender as he took his hands away.

"Well, we got a lot of work done…" he said as if

that helped excuse the way they'd just spent the last forty-five minutes.

"The whole place," she added with her own sort of validation. She knew that she should reprimand him for the make-out session and make it clear that it was never to happen again. But how could she do that when she'd been so completely indulgent and equally onboard and was—at that moment—just wanting to do it all again? And more…

"We should probably call it a night, though," she suggested then, before the restart that she was picturing went any further than her imagination. "It's late. I'm coming in tomorrow with furniture so I'll clean up better then."

He didn't argue with that. As they both got to their feet, he said, "Come on, I'll walk you to your car. You never know—maybe Merritt has become a more dangerous place after dark than it used to be."

The very notion of that made Marli smile. "Yeah, you never know."

They turned off all the office lights, went out and she locked the door behind them.

"Thanks for the help and the pizza," she said as they went to where her car and his truck were parked side-by-side just beyond the front door.

"That's what the marines are for."

"Painting and pizza?"

He chuckled. "Among a few other things… Didn't you know rolling paint on a wall was lesson one in basic training? Just like in *The Karate Kid.* That's why I can do it and you can't."

"Ah, no wonder," she played along with the feeble jest as they reached the driver's door of her sedan and she opened it.

But she didn't get in. She was just so reluctant to have him go even then. Instead she looked up at him again. At that face that was too handsome to be true. At those matchless blue eyes. At those lips...

And then he was kissing her once more, exactly the way she'd wanted—lips parted, tongues fencing, hinting at where things could go between them with just a little encouragement, his hands on the side-swells of breasts eager for it all to go further...

Before he stopped abruptly, took a step back and joked, "Careful of the traffic home."

"You, too," she said, finally getting into her car.

He shut her door firmly, tapped one knuckle against the window and went around to his truck.

There were no other vehicles on Independence or on any of the roads home so he was right behind her the entire way. That made it difficult for her not to keep glancing in her rearview mirror at him even as she told herself not to. It was equally difficult not to fantasize about him following her all the way into her driveway at home and then into the cottage...

Which of course he didn't do. They parted ways when she pulled into hers and he pulled into his in the opposite direction.

But still Marli took with her thoughts of the day, the evening, that make-out session…

You're playing with fire and you know you shouldn't…she told herself as she let herself into the cottage. She couldn't resist one last glance over her shoulder in hopes that Dalton might be just coming around the house to go in with her.

But the coast was clear and she went in alone, knowing without a doubt that it was for the best.

And still—in spite of that—wishing that Dalton might appear because she was longing for so much more of what had been last night and tonight.

For so much more of him…

Chapter Seven

"Hi. I'm stuck behind the one-ten," Dalton informed Marli on his cell phone.

"Oh, I forgot about that. I must have gotten over the tracks just in time. Sorry that you'll have to wait through it. I'll go ahead and get started putting away the tarps and cleaning up from last night—"

"I can walk faster than this thing is moving. But I'll be there when it finally passes. And just so you know, old man Johnson still moves his herd across the road to his other field when the train is going through."

"Ohhh," Marli groaned in sympathy. "Roll up your windows and close your vents—you know how much dung gets dropped along the way."

"Ah, country joys…" Dalton said facetiously. "I'll

be there eventually," he reiterated, ending the call and setting his phone on the passenger seat.

The coal train came through Merritt at approximately ten minutes after one on the third Friday of every month—hence why locals had come to call it the one-ten. If you got stuck behind it, there was no way around it and nothing to do but wait it out. Dalton did take Marli's advice, though, rolling up his window and closing his vents.

Then he draped both wrists over the top of the steering wheel as he watched the cows cross the road as slowly as the fully loaded train cars lumbering by. It was almost as if they were in sync.

The back of the Camden family truck that Dalton was using while he was home was loaded with Marli's office furniture. While performing his informal surveillance of Holt this morning, he'd spotted Marli loading things from the Abbott garage into the trunk of her car. It had reminded him that she'd mentioned she was going to bring furniture to her office today.

He hadn't thought about it until spotting her, but when he'd realized she had nothing but her sedan for transport, it had occurred to him that he had use of the truck. Like yesterday, he had nothing much to do and the availability of his grandfather to keep an eye on the Abbott house for him.

Why not help her out, he'd asked himself, finding the idea decidedly alluring—it was probably the first time since the dawn of man that anyone had ever found the idea of helping someone move to be a turn-on.

He'd recognized that that meant the true allure was in having an excuse to spend today with Marli.

Which he told himself also meant he shouldn't make the offer.

Tossing and turning through the night, he'd recognized that what was going on between them was not good.

Or actually, it was *too* good.

Kissing, full-on making-out to the point of starting to think about laying her down on that office carpet and finishing things, had been about as ill-advised as anything he'd ever done. His relationship with Marli had run its course and ended ugly years before, so there was nothing dumber than spending any time with her, let alone kissing her and stirring up ideas of more than that.

When it came to ended relationships he never went back. If something didn't work out the first time, it sure as hell wasn't going to work out the second time.

So what was happening between them shouldn't be fostered or facilitated. And he definitely shouldn't put himself back in the path of temptation. He'd learned in the last two nights that he couldn't trust himself with her.

He'd reminded himself of it all this morning as he'd watched her try to force office paraphernalia into her car. Offering to help her move, to set up her office today, would obviously be fostering and facilitating his feelings for her, which was the exact opposite of what he needed to do. So he'd ordered himself not to do it.

Then he'd seen Yancy Coltrain arrive at the Abbott house. In Coltrain's truck.

And even though Coltrain had parked in front of the house rather than pulling back to where Marli was, even though Holt came out of the house as if to greet a visitor so there was no indication that Coltrain was there for Marli, Dalton had been dialing her number to offer the Camden truck and his own help before Coltrain might have the chance.

"You are a damned disciplined member of the United States armed forces," he said out loud to himself as the train and cattle still meandered in front of him. "Put some of that into practice!"

At least put it into practice going forward—getting through today and from here on out.

But he *did* owe her for the acupuncture stuff, he thought. That *was* her occupation and what she got paid to do. And it had actually helped. So she had some compensation coming and this could be considered that, couldn't it?

"You're rationalizing, marine," he argued with himself, aware that the side of him that wanted to be with her was a more persuasive force than the side of him that knew better.

A more persuasive force but not a life-altering force...

When that crossed his mind he decided to take a closer look at the situation that way.

What was he thinking when he imagined being with her, kissing her, more than kissing her?

The answer to that was that he was only thinking about the urges he had.

But when he was trying *not* to think about her and he forced himself to think about the decision he'd come here to make, he did manage to switch gears effectively.

In fact, this morning when he'd made himself a cup of pre-dawn coffee and done a reread of the guidelines, regulations and possible sentences at each level of whatever charges he could press against Holt, it had occurred to him that spending so much time with Marli was actually giving him a cooler head—the way a good R and R could. And coming at any military decision with a cool head was what he wanted, even if that was not very easy for him when it involved Holt Abbott.

Marli *had* always had a tempering effect on him when it came to her brother. And since he didn't want to make this decision about Holt's career in anger, that was helpful. Not because she colored his decision, but because the clearheadedness she inspired in him gave him the ability to make this judgment call objectively.

But which factor was more important? The way Marli cooled his head…or the way she was heating him up in other regards?

"Man, you are just all over the place," he criticized himself.

But those "other regards" still popped back into his mind.

The kissing. The making out…

There was definitely heat between them.

Plenty of it.

And not just from him. She was as into it as he was, he thought, glancing as far down the tracks as he could and still seeing nothing but heavily laden coal car after coal car.

He'd ended the first kiss the night before last *and* the make-out session last night. If he hadn't he didn't know that she would have because there were no signs that she wasn't willing for things to go further.

How far, though, he asked himself.

The physical seemed possible. But beyond that?

He knew that *he* wasn't thinking about anything long-term, anything beyond this limited time here.

Was she?

She wasn't on a hunt for a man—she'd made that abundantly clear last night. She was trying to figure out if she was even suited for a long-term relationship with anyone. But she'd been onboard for what had happened between them the last two nights— onboard enough to not stop it herself.

So maybe she was in the same place he was—just living in the moment. The moment when they'd managed to put aside everything outside of them like they always had before. The moment when they'd become comfortable with each other again. When they were enjoying each other's company in a way that was a combination of the old and the new.

Was that so bad, as long as they were on the same page? As long as she wasn't balking or pushing him away?

If she did hesitate in the slightest he'd stop. Then he really would put that military discipline to work.

But otherwise?

Otherwise the R and R was nice. It was calming down his temper, his rage at Holt. It was letting him think more lucidly.

Being with her again, not hating her, not resenting her, not being so pissed off at her that he could hardly see straight, was also nice.

Catching up with her, finding out what she'd been up to for the last seventeen years was nice.

And kissing her?

"Whew…"

Kissing her was better than kissing anyone else had ever been…

So maybe he'd just play things by ear. Go with the flow. Make sure that the military discipline was close at hand, ready to be implemented at a split-second's notice if there was any indication that it needed to be.

But otherwise?

A little mostly-down-time at home to clear his head, do what he'd come here to do, put the rancid parts of his past with Marli behind him, and in the process getting some rest and recreation?

How was there anything bad about that?

You're playing with fire... Marli mentally repeated to herself, just as she had the night before.

The night before, when she'd come home hoping that Dalton might follow her to the cottage and come inside with her.

Now here she was, at five forty-five on Friday, having made sure that would happen.

She'd been surprised that he'd shown up to paint on Thursday, and surprised again to get his call this morning offering his truck to move furniture. But she wasn't about to say no—who would say no to that kind of help?

Not someone who needed to open her business as soon as possible so she could begin to generate some sorely missed income.

And—being honest with herself—not someone who had spent into the wee small hours of the morning reliving every minute of the day and evening she'd spent with Dalton...

Not someone who—despite trying to fight it—just wanted to be with him again.

So of course she'd said yes.

And they really had accomplished a lot. They made such a good team that between the two of them they'd succeeded not only in getting all of her office furniture and equipment into town but had also managed to completely arrange her office waiting room, situate her acupuncture tables in the treatment rooms and build the new wooden cabinets for her files as well as the new shelves and stands for her equipment and books. Dalton had even gotten her sound system to work so she could have the soft, soothing relaxation music she liked piped into both treatment rooms with just the flick of a switch.

After all that it had only seemed fair to once more compensate him for his work and she'd spontaneously invited him to the cottage for a home-cooked dinner.

Lemon chicken, asparagus drenched in butter and garnished with bacon, a salad, ciabatta bread, and chocolate crème brûlée for dessert.

It was only when the cooking was well underway—everything done that needed careful monitoring, leaving her free to hop into the shower—that it occurred to her what she'd put into play tonight.

Dalton was coming to the cottage for dinner...

After they'd kissed.

After they'd made out.

Marli had always been spontaneous, adventurous. That had changed somewhat when she'd found herself out in the world and susceptible to all of its dangers without Dalton there to watch her back. She had, over time, learned to be more cautious, more careful. But it was still in her nature to leap first, look second.

And tonight that's what she'd done in inviting him here before thinking about it, about the possible consequences of having him over for a very private dinner in her very small cottage. The past two days had already shown the mischief they might get up to if they were left alone together. And after already having spent another day together that had made work fun, a day in which they'd done more reminiscing, more laughing, more sharing, more reconnecting...

She'd leaped in.

Without looking.

Not wise...

Not difficult to understand, though, she thought as she shampooed her hair.

Getting to know Dalton as an adult, with even more strength and veracity and wisdom and insight and life experiences than he'd had when they were kids, just gave her more things about him to like, to be attracted to.

But liking him was one thing, being attracted to him was something else—that was the fire she was playing with. And it was turning into more and more of a blaze because she was attracted to him on a whole new level that hadn't even existed when they were both naive, curious kids.

And now Dalton was coming to the cottage for dinner...

The tiny cottage where her bedroom was right off the single room that provided a combination living, kitchen and dining area.

The tiny cottage where they would be entirely alone and undisturbed.

Where she was thinking about dressing in a sexy sundress.

Where, if tonight was anything like the last two nights and something got started between them, it would just be too easy and too convenient for it to escalate without interference and move to the bedroom.

Which made having this cozy little dinner in the cottage risky.

Very risky...

"But what are you going to do now?" she asked herself as she stepped out of the shower. "Are you going to call him and say *thanks for the help but I changed my mind about dinner, stay home...*"

Of course she couldn't do that. And when she'd made the offer to cook, she'd mentioned that she'd already had too many meals out lately, so she couldn't try switching to meeting him at a restaurant instead.

But the cottage was so small.

And the bedroom was so close.

And she was enjoying every minute with him more than she should have been.

And that make-out session last night was right at

the forefront of her mind no matter how much she tried to push it away...

It would be better if they could eat outside, she thought. Somewhere that was at least more in the open.

But the cottage was only separated from the main house by a small patch of cement—barely enough room for a café table and two chairs. If she *had* a café table or chairs, which she didn't.

Plus eating there would put them within feet of the kitchen where Holt and Bridget would have their own dinner tonight. Even if she did have a way to arrange for outside dining it would end up putting the two of them under Holt's scrutiny. In all likelihood, he'd provoke Dalton and make *that* situation worse.

And the only thing behind the cottage was a big oak tree with a treehouse in it...

The treehouse?

Marli bent over to blow-dry her hair from the bottom up, and considered what seemed like a silly notion.

But maybe a *workable* silly notion...

The last family to rent the house had had three young daughters. The father had asked for permission to refurbish the existing treehouse to give them a space to play in, to have sleepovers in.

She and Holt had given consent, imagining that it would involve only a replacement of the plywood floor, the four plywood sides, and either a less frayed rope ladder or a new one made of wooden slats.

But when Marli had arrived to check out the state of the cottage, she'd found that the artistry that the tenant had used to remodel and greatly improve the cottage had also gone into substantial changes to the treehouse.

For starters, there was a winding staircase complete with spindled balusters that replaced the rope ladder she and Holt had used. Once she'd seen that, she'd had to investigate further. She'd discovered that the staircase led to a cedar-walled tree chalet at least three times the size of what had been there before, with a steep roof that reached up into the branches.

Curious about the inside, she'd climbed the staircase and found that rather than getting to the hole in the floor that required the enterer to hoist themselves through, there was a carved—but only about five-foot high—door to enter.

The interior was a beautifully crafted tree-haven complete with a floor constructed of smooth, varnished planks. There were shelves on either side of the entrance; a narrow, built-in seat along one of the walls; a small drop-down table and drop-down benches on another of the walls; and an eight-inch step on the third side that expanded the space into another platform where Marli imagined three little girls' sleeping bags could be set side-by-side.

Lining the inside of the steeply slanted roof were

strings of white ball lights to add illumination in the dark, and when Marli had located the ends of them and plugged them into the power strip that connected to an outlet on the outside of the cottage, she'd found that the lights still worked.

Taking inventory of it in her mind now as she turned off the hairdryer and went on to scrunch the wavy length of her auburn hair, she recalled that the treehouse needed to be swept of leaves that had gathered in it, that Dalton would have to duck fairly far over to get through the doorway. Not to mention, he was too big to sit on any of the seating or to get his long legs under the miniature table. But with the drop-downs left up, the center space was expansive enough for the two of them to sit on the floor with the bench seat as a backrest. She could set their food on the sleeping platform, and they could picnic on the floor.

It wasn't ideal but it wasn't any more inconvenient than eating on the floor of her office had been. And the more she considered the treehouse, the more advantageous it seemed. Yes, it would be close quarters, but that also meant that it would be too close for them to stretch out—should anything seem to lead to that. And it was more of the kind of lark they'd gone on when they were young, as opposed to having dinner alone in the cottage, which would make it feel like a date.

So the treehouse it was, Marli decided, knowing

she had to hurry to give herself time to get ready and still be able to clean it and spruce it up.

With that in mind, she applied date makeup—feeling safer in prettying herself up now that she thought she'd taken the rest of the date-ishness out of tonight.

The sundress was definitely not right for sitting on the floor of the treehouse so she bypassed that and chose black jeans with a black and white zebra print top.

The top was silky, and because the shoulders were cut-in, she couldn't wear a separate bra so the knit shelf bra inside had to be enough. But even though it left her shoulders beguilingly bare, she thought that the demure mock-neck made it only semi-sexy and not altogether accessible—a fair trade-off for the sundress.

She also decided not to leave her hair down and instead twisted it back, fastening it with a plastic chopstick and leaving just a spray of curls at her crown because that seemed more functional and less engaging.

Then she slipped her feet into a simple pair of black ballet flats, checked on the chicken in the oven, and went out to the treehouse, knowing that neither Clint nor Nolan nor Arnie would have gone along with this idea.

And just hoping that Dalton would prove to be different from them all.

* * *

"The doorway is a little short so you'll have to duck," Marli told Dalton as she led him up the tree-house stairs. "But once you get inside I think you'll be able to stand straight—at least in the middle."

Dalton laughed. "Dinner in a tree… I'll hand it to you, Abbott, you're still coming up with things no other woman I know would ever imagine."

He hadn't balked at her idea when she'd told him about the relocation of their dinner—citing the residual cooking heat in the cottage as the reason they should move outdoors.

"I think I was twelve the last time I was up here… it's a little different…" he noted as she took a tray of food inside and he followed her with a bottle of wine and two glasses.

He did have to bend over to get through the doorway but once inside he gingerly straightened to his full height with enough space to spare to not put the strings of lights in jeopardy.

"What do you think?" Marli asked as she set the tray on the sleeping platform.

He glanced around them. "I've been barracked in worse. I think it'll work," he said.

"We'll have to eat picnic style on the floor…"

"Again—I've eaten in worse ways…without all these big pillows around."

She'd taken several oversized, plush velvet throw pillows off her bed for them to sit on.

"So you're game?"

"Sure," he said as if he didn't know why he wouldn't be.

Marli couldn't help smiling at that, unable to picture any of her three fiancés taking this as amiably. She appreciated that flexibility and open-mindedness in Dalton. "Then why don't you open the wine while I get the rest of our dinner?"

"Can I help?" he asked.

"There's a pulley system attached to a box down below—between that and one more tray I think I can get everything. If you just deal with the wine we'll be all set."

"Holler when you have the box loaded and I'll pull it up."

"Will that hurt your shoulder?" she asked. He'd already told her much earlier that her treatment had been helpful but she didn't want him to overtax it.

"Strange as it seems to me, it's like I never strained it, so I don't see any problem."

"If you're sure…"

"I am. Just holler," he said again.

"Okay, then. Be right back," Marli said, going around him to return to the door.

As she did she couldn't help stealing another secret glance at him. He was wearing a pair of jeans with a navy blue polo shirt. The clothes looked new and fitted him so well it was abundantly clear how lean and toned and muscular he was—in fact, the short sleeves of the polo shirt could barely stretch far enough to wrap his biceps and there was no bagginess across his chest or shoulders, either.

His hair was shiny-clean, there was a shadow of scruff still on his face that looked precision-trimmed and supple. He looked so well put together that she had the impression that she hadn't been the only one of them to have been headed into tonight as if it were a date.

So all the better that she'd moved their dinner outside, she told herself, confident that it had been the safer choice.

"You learned to cook," Dalton observed half an hour later when they'd begun to eat the meal she'd prepared. He'd already complimented her on the food, not veiling his surprise.

By then they were sitting comfortably on the pillows, backs against more pillows, plates on their laps and glasses of wine waiting alongside them.

"Yes, I did," Marli said, not taking any offense at the history tucked behind the comment. "I know it must come as a shock. It certainly seemed to me like it might never happen after all those burned dinners I made when my mom couldn't make herself get out of bed for weeks on end."

"And after setting your kitchen stove on fire," Dalton reminded.

"That's what happens when an inexperienced ten year old tries to make grilled cheese sandwiches.

Eventually I got the hang of it, though—especially once I was living on my own and on a budget too tight to afford eating out. On my second trip to Europe, I even took some short cooking classes—I learned to bake bread in Paris."

He held up his slice of ciabatta and raised inquiring eyebrows at her to ask if she'd made that.

"No, I didn't have time to make bread today—but the general store has done pretty well keeping up with the times so they have a *lot* more choices than there ever were when we were kids, including that."

He nodded, finished what he'd been chewing and said, "You took cooking classes in *Paris*?"

"And one in Italy to learn how to make homemade pasta, and two in the states for more general things."

"I would never have guessed that was something you'd do. I mean, the food is great, but you never seemed to be interested in cooking."

"I've taken a lot of classes over the years—outside of college and acupuncture-related coursework—just to learn how to do new things."

"Such as?"

"Some of them were practical, like everyday car maintenance and repair. Home repair. I also took some classes on painting—pictures not walls, and before you ask, what I learned most was that I don't have any talent. Not in painting or pottery or jewelry-making, either. But I can make some nice candles. I'm not bad at archery or target shooting. I learned how to train service animals but never got to do it because I couldn't fit it into my schedule. I'm a master gardener—something I'll be able to do more of here. I can play a decent bridge game, a better poker game, and I went to school to learn to deal cards so I could work weekends in an Atlantic City casino as a second job before my acupuncture practice in New York earned enough to pay the bills. I've taken dance lessons so I can waltz, fox trot, tango—you name it. Oh, and chess—I took a class in that and I dare you to try and beat me now." Something he'd done frequently long ago.

Dalton laughed again. "You weren't kidding when you said you wanted to experience everything. You're very accomplished," he teased mildly.

"How about you—any extra-curriculars?"

"Mine have all been called training and they don't make for interesting dinner conversation."

"How about travel? Where have you been in the world?"

"In the States, only to military bases, wherever trainings or maneuvers are held, or where natural disasters have happened. Outside of the country, a lot of places in the Middle East. I've been to China and Japan, too. Africa and South America. I used leave time over the years to see most of Europe. I've been to Russia and Poland. I haven't been to Canada or Australia—"

"I haven't been to Australia, either," Marli said,

inclined to follow it with *maybe we could go together* but she stopped short and reminded herself that there was no relationship between them that might accommodate that.

"Will you take a class in the care and feeding of kangaroos before you go?" he teased her.

"I might, you never know."

He smiled at that then complimented her again on the food as he cleaned his plate.

Marli had also had enough so she set their dishes out of the way on the platform and got their dessert while Dalton topped off their wine.

"This looks decadent," he said of the chocolate crème brûlée.

"It is," she assured. "Dark and decadent with a hint of brandy in the brown sugar that I torched on the top like a welder."

He cracked the caramelized topping and tried it, letting his eyes roll back into his head after his first bite. "Oh, yeah…" he groaned in compliment. "That is good stuff! Paris?"

"I actually learned that recipe in Chicago," she corrected, enjoying hers, too. Then, as they settled into that last course she said, "When can we get into the juicy parts of your life?"

"The juicy parts?" he repeated.

"Girlfriends… Relationships… We got into mine last night. And you dropped a little bombshell I've been wondering about ever since. So spill," she commanded.

"I don't remember dropping a bombshell. Honestly, there's not much to tell."

"Oh, come on," she cajoled. "You became a marine not a priest." And all she had to do was look at him to know he had to have had plenty of opportunities with women.

"You don't become a major at my age and have a booming personal life."

"Holt was right behind you on the track to becoming a major and he still had time for more women than I could keep up with before he met Bridget. Don't act like your job meant that you've had to behave like a choirboy."

"Well you know I could never sing," he joked. "But I don't really have *relationships*."

"Does that mean you just play around a lot?"

"No," he said as if she were insulting him. "I just… I put everything into being a marine and when I have some R and R…" He shrugged, finishing his crème brûlée and accepting the other half of hers when she silently offered it. "There's usually interest in a few hours or days of time together with someone before we go back to our regularly scheduled lives."

He was obviously reluctant to talk about this. Which only whetted Marli's appetite all the more. "You grew up to be a womanizing dog?" she challenged.

"No," he refuted with more force. "I meet women, sometimes we hit it off—not anyone under my command because that's fraternizing and against regulations. But women who are like me, who aren't looking for anything more than a short weekend trip or a couple of days of…semi-hibernation together… With women who agree they don't want anything more than that—there *are* those, you know."

"Do you remember their names when it's over?" Marli goaded.

"It's never just a pick-up. It's always someone I know, who knows me, who's on the same page I am, so yeah, I know their names."

Marli was gripped by this subject but still finding it difficult to hear about. Somehow, it was even worse than talking about her own past relationships the night before. It had been embarrassing to admit the ways in which all her engagements had fallen apart, but to think of Dalton with other women was something else. And telling herself she wasn't allowed to have a double standard didn't stop it—she realized she would have preferred to learn that their one time together had been his *only* time. Even if that was absurdly unrealistic.

Still, she pushed on to the even bigger question. "The bombshell you dropped the other night was when you said you *almost* got married once," she reminded him.

"That was early on…" he said as if it didn't count,

finishing the dessert and setting the dish on the platform with all of their discards. Then he picked up his wineglass and angled his body toward her, rolling partially onto one hip, bending one knee to give his arm a resting place.

"Early or not you *almost* got *married*," she persisted. "When? Who? What did you *think better of* not to go through with it?" she finished.

He took a drink of his wine and kept his eyes on the glass as he answered. "*When* was right out of the academy during first year marine training. *Who* was Bella Williams, a training officer's daughter. And I'm pretty sure the mess I made was your fault," he ended, calling back to her words to him the previous evening when she'd blamed him for her relationship failures.

"My fault?" she said, needing more of an explanation.

"I think I asked her to marry me as a really delayed rebound," he said solemnly, with regret in his voice, staring into his wine. "I didn't have anything to do with anyone romantically after you left town, and at the academy I buried myself in classes and trainings and anything I could do to shut off my head. But my brothers pressured me into taking Bella to the Ring Dance—"

"I know about that from Holt—it's almost as big a deal as a presidential inaugural ball."

He nodded. "It is. It's at the end of junior year,

you get your class ring after it's dipped in water from the seven seas. Formal, ceremonial—it's big. And it calls for a date. Bella's dad wasn't my training officer then, but he was on campus and he and his family lived close by. My brothers had met Bella around—at parties, clubs. They forced me to go out with them one night to introduce us. She was okay…" He shrugged. "So I asked her to the dance and she said yes—an invitation to the Ring Dance rarely gets turned down. Anyway, we went, had a nice enough time, and I just thought that was it." Another shrug of those shoulders that were so, so wide and strong…

Marli corralled her wandering mind and said, "But that wasn't it?"

"She kind of kept coming after me—calling, getting her friend to convince my brothers to bring me with them when they were all going out. It went on through senior year, sort of evolved on its own into a relationship even though I wasn't really trying for one," he said without much enthusiasm. "Bella was cute, sweet, we had a good time together. Then I graduated and went into training with her old man and…" Yet another shrug. "I just sort of found myself in my first full-blown relationship after you. And it was okay, for the most part. Then I got this idea…"

He seemed very reluctant to get it all out.

Afraid she might say something wrong, Marli left him to it, encouraging him by not filling the gap his pause left.

Finally, he came out with it. "God, I was young… just a kid still…and I got this idea that marriage was the best way to make sure she stuck around…"

After I hadn't… Marli thought, sad that he'd felt the need to ensure that. "So you *wanted* her to stick around. You *did* have feelings for her…" she said tentatively, unwilling—unable—to add weight by calling what he had shared with Bella "love." She couldn't tolerate thinking about it that way.

"I…" He shook his head and his expression was one of confusion. And guilt. "I don't know. The more time I spent with Bella, the more I got used to being with someone again. She was available whenever I wanted her to be, she was someone to be a couple with, to hang out with when there was no one else." He grimaced. "Geez, that sounds bad… But I liked her, I was comfortable with her, she was understanding of the whole military thing, patient with the extra trainings I signed up for and then just really happy with whatever time I gave her. She was always telling me how much I meant to her, how she never wanted it to end—all that kind of stuff that fed my ego. I think I needed that after what had gone on here."

"That does sound rebound-ish," Marli said, beginning to feel guilty again herself. It was seeming more and more like he was right—this might have been her fault for the way she'd left him, hurt him. "So you proposed?" she asked carefully.

"Bella talked about getting married pretty often

so there was no question that that was what she wanted. I knew she was clear on what being a military wife meant. She was willing to have the life her mother had had, raise kids the way her mother had—with a frequently absent father. I started thinking that yeah, it might be okay to have someone to come home to after being deployed, someone I knew would be there because she didn't really want to be anywhere else…"

"So you proposed and she jumped at the idea," Marli guessed.

"Yeah," Dalton said, sounding all the more guilty.

"But you couldn't go through with it."

"I didn't want to hurt her but the closer the wedding day got, the closer I looked at my feelings for her and realized they were pretty superficial. They weren't the feelings I should have had for someone I was supposed to spend the rest of my life with. I started asking myself what the hell I was doing—"

"Because it wasn't right."

"Because she wasn't you," Dalton said frankly, putting his wineglass on the platform as if he was finished with it. When he'd done that he settled back the way he'd been positioned before, but now he rested his arm on top of the bench seat and finally looked her in the eye.

"I think I may have needed just to know that I *could* get the girl. But in the end I couldn't escape the fact that it was the wrong way, the wrong reason, to go into a marriage—I was young but I did finally get a grip and see that. So I called it off. And then took retribution on the training field from her father. The man damn near killed me," he finished with some levity. Marli was glad that he could joke about it now, but she didn't believe that was how he'd seen it at the time.

"Again… I'm sorry," she said.

"You might owe that apology to Bella."

"Should I look her up?" Marli asked in her own attempt to lighten the tone.

"She lives in Maryland, she's married to a dentist, has four kids," he said, almost sounding like he really did want her to reach out and get in touch.

But Marli knew him well enough to see the glint of mischief in those dazzling blue eyes that told her he was kidding. So she just tossed the ball back into his court. "On the other hand, I'll bet by now when she tells that story she says she almost married a jerk and then found the real love of her life and she's glad it happened."

"I don't know… I ran into her a couple of years ago. After all this time, I thought maybe we could look at it as a lucky escape for both of us. At the very least, I figured we could be civil, and I could apologize again without having a book thrown at my head. But when I said hello to her she slapped me across the face, called me a bastard and told me I had a lot of gall to go anywhere near her. Call me silly but I think there are hard-feelings…"

"Yeah, I'd say…" Marli agreed.

She'd had enough wine so she reached over him to set her glass on the platform behind him.

She managed to do it without making physical contact but when she sat back again she found herself unwittingly closer to him. She was worried he might think she'd done it on purpose so she sat facing him rather than resting her back against the bench again. She crossed her legs in front of her as a bit of a distance-keeper and forced herself to ignore the thought of how much she would like to have settled in next to him, maybe inspired him to put his arm around her…

"So ever since then—all the rest of these years—you've just left it at playing around?" she asked then.

"After the mess with Bella I swore off women again for a while, until I was sure my head was on right. I didn't want to cause anything like that with anyone else. I regrouped, got a clear idea of where my priorities were, and since *then* I've been dedicated to being a marine. That's what gets my all. I'm happy with my personal life taking a backseat to it, happy with the fact that when there's time there's always someone with some interest in nothing but a little fun, without anyone getting hurt."

"And that works for you? Just that for the sum and substance of your personal life?"

"So far, so good," he said.

"You don't care about not having someone to come home to?" Hadn't that been the reason he'd proposed to the other woman?

"There's been a few times when I've been the only one of my unit returning from somewhere who doesn't have anyone waiting to greet them and I feel it a little then," he admitted. "But after a mission, a deployment, I'm usually better winding down on my own anyway. And when I'm ready for company, I find it."

Marli didn't like the image of him returning to nothing while other people in his unit came back to loving families eager to welcome them home. "That's not what I want for you," she heard herself say.

He laughed. "What do you want for me?"

"You deserve to have open arms to come home to. Happy tears because it's so good to see you. Kids who run and jump for you to catch them and hold them tight, to smother you in hugs…"

"It's my choice, Marli," he reasoned. "My career comes first and foremost."

"But you're already a *major*… Your career is soaring. At this point, does it still need your full focus? If you don't pay some attention to the other part of your life now—when your head *is* on right—you'll be missing out on experiencing the best of what life has to offer. A genuine, close relationship, a family of your own—"

"I'm *experiencing* enough for me. You're the one of us obsessed with *experiencing* everything from soup to nuts. I'm okay with the way I'm going."

"No!" she insisted. "You were always right there with me to explore, to *experience* everything from soup to nuts, too. You can't just fob off your whole personal life now, you can't just reduce it to *recreation*."

"I don't need the distraction of it being anything more than that."

"But you'll end up a crusty old man, all alone!"

"Well, what about you? You think you might not be *cut out* for marriage, that it might be a *bad fit* for you, that maybe you aren't the *marrying kind*—if you stick with that don't you run the risk of ending up a crusty old *woman* all alone?" he volleyed back.

"I'm just figuring things out for myself. But even if marriage can't work out for me that doesn't mean I'm not still hoping there will be… I don't know… someone to share my life with, a relationship that I can count on in one form or another. I still want kids, family… I don't want a laundry list of disposable playmates who are never truly important to me. That's what you're describing and what you seem to be settling for."

"Are you about to tell me you have a friend who you know I'd be just right for? Because usually that kind of stuff leads to somebody trying to fix me up," he joked.

She shook her head, refusing to follow his lead in treating this like a joke. "I just don't want there to be any more fallout from what I did. I don't want to be to blame for you ending up alone and empty because *you're* too afraid of being left again," she said. As much as it was unbearable for her to think of him with someone else, it was worse to think of him never finding real happiness.

"I'm not afraid of anything, Marli," he said calmly, confidently enough for it not to be defensive, a simple statement of fact.

"I'm sure you believe that. Maybe you aren't afraid of what comes your way as a marine because you've trained for everything and because...well, look at you..." Which she did—at the awesome specimen he was. "I'm sure you can handle pretty much anything that life throws your way. But when it comes to a well-rounded, whole, complete life...you don't have one. And you need to."

He laughed again. "I'm fine, Marli," he said as if she was making too big a deal of this.

"You just think you are because it feels safe not to let anyone get close, so you don't have to worry about them leaving you hanging. The way I did..."

"Did you sign up for extra-curricular psych classes, too?" he said, not taking what she was saying to heart.

"I don't need an extra-curricular psych class on Dalton Camden," she persisted. "I know you, remember? You never pushed things too far with Holt even when he had it coming because he was my brother. You held back because he was my family and you said family was a big deal. *Your* family was important to you—even the Colorado Camdens you went to spend time with in the summers."

She realized she was picking up steam as she went, but she couldn't help it. "When I got pregnant you didn't freak out nearly as bad as I did—you just switched gears—you said us getting married, having the baby would be great, that a baby would make *us* a family. And even if you were just trying to put a positive spin on a difficult situation, I could tell you were more okay with it than I was *because* of the way you felt about family."

"Marli—"

She wasn't going to let him stop her before she was finished. "I don't believe that now having no family of your own, no one to come back to, doesn't bother you at all. Family meant enough to you years ago to ask that girl to marry you so you'd have someone to come home to. And now you're trying to pass it off as nothing to you? As if all you've ever wanted was to be a lone wolf? I'm not buying it!"

"You are all wound up about this—"

"Because it's important," she contended. "And I can't stand to think that what happened with us, what I did, might warp your whole life…"

"My life isn't *warped.* If I ever start to feel like I'm missing out I can always do something about it, can't

VICTORIA PADE 213

I? You've changed course, conventional stuff hasn't worked for you and you're trying to figure out what might, aren't you? I could always change course, too."

"But it's been what? *Twelve* years since that other girl? It seems like you're stuck…"

"I'm not stuck, I'm *fine* with the way things are," he emphasized.

"I'm worried you might let life pass you by," she said.

He laughed yet again but this time compassionately as he took her hand and held it. "Of course you are because that's *you,* Marli—always worried that life might pass *you* by. It was always your go-to reason when you were talking me into your wildest schemes—that I couldn't let life pass me by, and I'd always go along. But I don't feel like life or anything else is passing me by now. I'm absolving you of the past and of any responsibility for my decisions. It's my own fault. It's what I've chosen for myself," he reiterated. "The same as when I opted not to try riding the Huntszerger's bull when I was fifteen."

"It was fun—even if he did throw me off into the mud—and you missed it."

"He might have been too old to bother turning and trying to gore us, but he was still one hell of a good bucker and I had body parts that were becoming particularly important to me that I didn't want to risk," Dalton reminded with a smile.

"But I rode the bull and you didn't," she insisted.

"And I didn't regret it. Especially when you smelled the way you did all the way home. It wasn't *only* mud he threw you off into."

She smiled a little at the memory, but it faded quickly. She was still too concerned about Dalton denying himself all it seemed to her that he was denying himself to let him distract her. She held his eyes with her own as she returned to the real subject at hand. "Please don't let yourself have just half a life," she beseeched him, more aware than she wanted to be of how big and strong and warm—and good—it felt to have her hand still in his, to have his thumb rubbing the back of it.

"Don't worry about that," he countered, brushing her concern aside. Then he laughed again—this time with something in it that seemed sensual—and said, "As mad at you as I was, as mad at you as I've been for so many years, who would have thought I'd be here trying to get you to *not* take some blame?"

Still, she felt compelled to say, "Promise me that you won't settle…that superficial isn't all you ever let yourself have."

"I can only promise to do what works for me," he said honestly, sincerely, looking into her eyes. "And that I won't blame you if I regret it later on down the road."

But then, as if to prove he could go beyond the superficial, he leaned forward enough to kiss her a kiss that was anything but frivolous or insignificant.

A kiss that began as deeply as the previous evening's kiss had ended, with parted lips and little delay before the tongue she hadn't had enough of came to entice hers again.

Marli told herself that this was exactly what she'd been trying to avoid by relocating their dinner to the treehouse and that she should stop it.

You know you shouldn't be doing this.

But it didn't matter. Not when kissing him once more was as good as it was and answered a craving in her that was begging to be soothed.

And when the hand he wasn't holding rose to his chest to push him away, she found herself instead resting it in place so it could drink in the feel of his polo shirt over the steel of his muscles. From there, it went even higher to the side of his neck, to the back of his neck, curving around it to bring them closer still and deepen the kiss even more.

Her thoughts quieted and there was nothing but Dalton and that kiss, nothing but their tongues challenging each other, meeting every challenge and starting another.

His arm moved from the bench seat to come around her, pulling her nearer. He brought their clasped hands up to the center of his pecs where he let go of hers to find one of her bare shoulders instead. Meanwhile, his right hand began to work her back in a firm, kneading massage.

It didn't happen all at once but after some time of

just kissing him, just having his hands where they were, Marli began to crave even more. Her breasts seemed to swell against the fabric of the shelf bra, straining toward him, eager for his attention.

And if that wasn't enough, she sent the hand caught between their bodies around him, lessening the space between them and moving on to explore the expanse of his broad shoulders.

As if that gave him more license, he pulled her forward even farther, enough for her legs to be forced to uncross and go to one side, putting her on her hip, their body positions mirrored. He brought her up close enough for her breasts to barely brush his chest. No more than that was called for to inspire her nipples to swell and pebble, responsive and ready for more contact.

Dalton always had been able to read her and that was when his right hand came from her shoulder to the side of one increasingly engorged breast, pausing and finding his invitation in Marli making way for him.

That big hand went to her breast then, outside of the silky blouse, and she suddenly regretted tucking the hem into her jeans. But it seemed too blatant a clue to tug it out herself so instead she sent the message by locating the end of his shirt and sliding both of her hands under it to his naked back.

Dalton didn't reciprocate for a time but it didn't matter—she still had his hand on her breast even if it *was* outside of her clothes—and now she got to feel the splendor of satin skin taut over massive muscles, of shoulders too wide to be real.

He repositioned them until leaning on their hips became partially lying down. The dimensions of the floor space that didn't allow for stretching out but did allow for a semi-recline, cushioned by the throw pillows.

Kissing turned into a passionate pillage of mouths and Dalton finally responded to what Marli had been signaling—he eased her blouse out of her waistband and brought his so-talented hand underneath it to rediscover her unrestrained breast.

That first touch of his warm hand on her yearning flesh caused her breath to catch slightly in her throat and took her instantly from craving to full, uncontrolled, demanding turn-on, resulting in her bringing one of her legs over his and her lower half fully against him.

An almost silent moan rumbled from him and he shifted his body over her a bit more, making her wonder just how much they might be able to do in that small space even without completely stretching out.

Or they could go inside…

Marli tried hard to fight that idea but his hand was doing amazing things to her breasts, his thick thigh was high between her legs right where she needed pressure the most, and she wanted him too much to win that battle between common sense and need.

She was going to take him inside, into the cottage, to her double bed and not a single thing beyond getting him there had any importance at all.

And then out of the blue he stopped.

He took his hand from under her blouse as if her breast had burned it.

He abandoned her mouth.

He yanked his head back with force and when Marli opened her eyes she saw that his were closed tight, lines of stress drawn into his sculpted face. He was holding his breath and his sharp jaw was clenched, all in what appeared to be a battle with himself until, finally, he seemed to achieve some control.

He exhaled, untensed somewhat, opened his blue eyes and brought them to hers again. "I want this like nothing I've ever wanted before..." he said in a voice as ragged as he looked. "But not until you've cooled down enough to think it through...completely through. I'm not here much longer, I don't know when we'll see each other again after I leave. You have to be clear that this is *only* about right now, only about you and me, nothing else."

In other words, just another hookup, like all his other hook-ups.

Okay!

That was Marli's first thought. Anything was okay if she could just go on with this, if she could just have him in her bed...in her body...

Even if it was only for now…

But then reason finally set in and she knew he was right to force her to really consider it. Right and unwavering because she could hear in his voice that nothing could persuade this new, tower-of-strength Dalton to go on anyway.

Then he slid her up to sit against the front of the bench seat and sat upright himself, bending one long leg between them to recreate some distance.

"We're not just picking up where we left off, Marl," he said, using the nickname he'd favored when they were at the height of their buddy phase. "I have a job to do here. I'll go back to my life when I've done it." It was a warning but it came with a regret that softened it. "You gotta keep that in mind."

"I know," she whispered, telling herself that she was grateful for the reminder to get herself under control.

"Maybe that doesn't matter," he said hopefully. "But I don't want you doing anything you might regret if it does…"

Her safety net yet again…

She nodded reluctant agreement. "It's probably better if you get out of here, though," she warned, despite all she really wanted still was to grab his hand and not let go until she had him in her bedroom.

He didn't say anything and merely reached out to run the backs of his fingers down her cheek in a feather-light stroke. He paused part-way and lingered as if the need to stay, to kiss her and go on to even more, was hitting him again. Hard enough to cup her shoulder with his other hand once more, to squeeze it, to pull her a scant fraction of an inch toward him as if temptation was winning...

Until he took his hands away, stood, ducked through that abbreviated treehouse door and disappeared down the stairs.

Marli sat there, listening to every step he took, knowing he was doing exactly what he should be doing for them both, what she should have had the strength to do for herself.

But whether it was right, reasonable, rational or not, she just wanted him so much it had been impossible for her to say no and not allow herself to experience him...

Just one more time...

Chapter Eight

"Now what?" Ben Camden asked Dalton as he returned to the kitchen and the breakfast he and his grandfather were in the middle of on Saturday morning. The meal had been interrupted twice—first there had been a phone call Dalton had had to take and then a knock on the front door by a uniformed marine.

Dalton had a large manila envelope in his hand that he set on the counter next to his cell phone. "That was the delivery of Holt's service record to go along with the colonel's call telling me to get my ass in gear."

"And court-martial Holt," Ben contributed.

"That's what the colonel and the Senator want, yeah. And they're tired of waiting."

"How about I make you more eggs? Those must be ice cold by now," Ben offered.

"Nah, that's all right. I'll eat these—they're still good even when they're cold," he assured his grandfather—which was nothing more than the simple truth. He couldn't get enough of the scrambled eggs full of peppers and onions and cheese and his grandfather's special seasonings.

"*Are* you closer to deciding?" Ben asked, his own breakfast plate cleaned, sitting back with his coffee cup in hand while Dalton ate.

"Closer and struggling with how far I'm leaning toward court-martial," he admitted. It was his decision to make, but his grandfather had always provided good counsel and maybe he could use a little of that.

The older man nodded solemnly.

It was that solemnity that spurred Dalton to defend himself. "I gave Holt a *direct order* not to vary from my course of action. He'd already crossed a line when he got in my face about how much better he could have planned the mission and how it *should* be done," he said emphatically.

Another solemn nod from the elderly man.

"He ignored the order! He put everyone in more danger—including the teenage hostages. It was a damn miracle that those girls weren't executed on the spot when Holt and his men set off that mine!"

"But they weren't and they—along with Holt and

his own men—all have you to thank that nothing even worse happened. Holt did what he always did when it came to you—he went to extremes to best you no matter the cost to everyone, including himself."

"Only this wasn't a schoolyard pissing contest—"

"It was serious business."

"It was more than serious business, it was a delicate, dangerous mission with high profile civilians involved," Dalton said with a full head of steam. "And that idiot couldn't seem to tell the difference between that and whatever the hell it is that gets into him when it comes to me!"

"So you're going to have him court-martialed," Ben concluded.

Even though Dalton was leaning in that direction he wasn't fully there. "I still have to go over Abbott's service record. I'm doing that today," he said in answer to his grandfather's statement.

"If you do have him court-martialed and he's convicted, what would his living conditions be like in confinement—and should you take that into consideration?" Ben asked.

"No, I can't take that into consideration any more than I could take it into consideration if he wore glasses. If he was to go into confinement whatever needs he has would be accommodated."

That must have sounded harsh to his grandfather because Ben recoiled slightly and his bushy white eyebrows arched high. But still he conceded, "You're within your rights. He likely *would* be convicted because there's no question he disobeyed your orders."

"But if you were on the jury—because after all, a general court-martial is just like a civil trial and there would be a jury—you'd vote against conviction," Dalton guessed.

"If I was on a jury, I still think I'd have to factor in that the consequences for his actions were mainly his own. That even though disobeying an order is a military crime, it still isn't a murder or a robbery or something. I don't think he needs to be removed from society because he's a danger to other people. Whether you push it or not, he'll be discharged so he won't be taking orders anymore from anyone—except maybe his wife and that just makes him her problem. And I'd be thinking about the long-range fall-out of a dishonorable discharge. I'd want to know if this was his only bad act, if there are good ones to outweigh it, or if there are a string of other things he's stepped over the line on. You boys have been in the service for a lot of years. I guess I'd want to know all the good and all the bad to decide what he deserves now, at the end of his career."

Signaling that he'd said his piece, Ben got up and took care of the breakfast dishes.

But as he did his words took some root with Dalton. He and Holt had crossed paths over the years at various bases, trainings, meetings, conferences, events. But until this Syria mission, they hadn't worked together, hadn't shared assignments or duties. He knew Holt had risen through the ranks almost as quickly as he had but he didn't actually know what had gone into that for Holt or what was in his service record, positive or negative.

Ben finished at the sink and came to push in his chair, standing behind it as Dalton sat back with his own coffee now and looked up at the elderly man.

"You know more about this than I do," Ben said. "And I wouldn't want to be in your shoes. No matter which way you go, you lose."

"How so?"

"If you don't court-martial him you'll end up on the wrong side of a colonel and a senator, and who knows what that could mean for your career. If you do court-martial Holt you'll lose the girl."

"Marli? Marli isn't mine *to* lose," Dalton said.

"You've been spending a lot of time with her again," the older man pointed out.

"Still, not mine to lose."

Ben nodded once more. "Maybe not. But if you ask me, she should be. I've never seen two people who belonged together more than the two of you—despite all the issues with that brother of hers."

"Once I've made this decision I'm back to my unit. It's been good to see her..." *So damn good...* "but it can't last, and that's all there is to it."

Another nod from his grandfather, this one slower

than the rest, with an air of patience, as if he knew better and was just waiting for Dalton to see the light.

But the older man didn't say more. Instead he switched gears. "Why don't you use my office today? My desk is clear, you can close the door, spread out, dig into that service record, watch the Abbott house from the window in there."

"Thanks, I'll do that," Dalton responded.

"And whatever you decide? I know it'll be the right thing," Ben said, his voice full of confidence in him.

"I'm trying to," Dalton muttered into his coffee cup as Ben headed out of the room.

He stood and took his own breakfast plate to the dishwasher then poured himself another cup of coffee, grabbed his phone and the manila envelope and went to Ben's office.

Along the way he kept thinking about what he'd said—that Marli wasn't his to lose. It was nothing more than the truth, and yet he felt a twinge at that knowledge.

Be glad that she isn't yours, he told himself, *if she was it would make this decision worse.*

But at least the fact that he didn't have anything to lose when it came to Marli meant his judgement on the court-martial issue wasn't clouded. He *was* glad of that. He'd meant it when he'd told her last night that he was fine with his personal life the way it was, with the marines being his priority. This was proof that his lack of ties outside of the marines freed him of conflicts that could have gotten in his way. It left him clearheaded.

So no, Marli wasn't his to lose and that was for the best.

For him and for her, too, since she was in some kind of limbo with her own relationship situation anyway and not looking to get into anything.

Big Ben was just waxing nostalgic when he said that the two of them belonged together.

And maybe he was getting lost in nostalgia, too, to have that twinge.

Although even if Marli was his to lose, a decision to court-martial Holt wouldn't necessarily mean that he would lose her. She had an admirable objectivity when it came to her brother. That's why she'd always given Dalton the heads-up when she found out that Holt was planning something. First she'd tried to talk Holt out of it. Failing that, she'd warn Dalton and let the chips fall where they might, regardless of the consequences for her pigheaded brother.

When it came to the potential court-martial, Dalton knew she was hoping for the best even as she'd respected his not-talking-about-it edict. His own grandfather had done more lobbying for leniency than Marli had, so once more she was being objective.

And considering that, it occurred to Dalton that he owed her that in return. That he had to let go of his feelings, his animosity toward Holt and look at him as just any other marine.

As Dalton closed the office door and situated himself behind the desk, he made a silent vow to Marli that he would follow the example she'd set. That he would not let his and Holt's bad history be a part of this decision any more than he would let being on good terms with Marli influence it.

He unsealed the envelope, took out the file and opened it to lay out in front of him.

Duty assignments.

Performance.

Awards and medals.

Disciplinary actions.

Administrative remarks.

Personnel actions.

"Let's see what you've got, Marine," he said to the papers in front of him, striving for that objectivity that Marli had modeled for him.

Despite how satisfying it might have been to have the last word with his old nemesis.

"Oh, for cripes' sake…now it's too high on your side again, Bridge. Isn't there a better way to do this?"

"No. Something is wonky when we go by the measurements. You have to eyeball it and just tell us when it *looks* right," Marli instructed her brother.

It was late Saturday afternoon and she and Bridget were hanging drapes over the living room window.

Marli was on a small ladder on one side, her sister-in-law was standing on a chair on the other end, and they'd assigned Holt the job of telling them when the top and bottom of the drapes appeared even.

Holt sighed but complied. "Okay, you dropped your end too far, Bridge. Bring it back up about half an inch... Ah, Marli, now your end slipped..."

"Let me switch arms," she suggested. Once she'd done that, she looked up and adjusted the bracket plate so it was in the place she'd marked with a pencil back when her brother had decided her end was at the right height.

"Okay, now you're too high, Bridget—"

But as Holt said that, movement outside caught Marli's eye and she glanced through a gap in the two drapery panels.

Dalton was walking up the driveway.

From the stiffness of his posture, the stern expression on his face, she could tell he wasn't coming to see her.

"Dalton's here..." she said.

Bridget instantly pulled the rod and drapes down to peer out the window and see for herself.

"He doesn't look happy..." she said, alarmed.

Her sister-in-law was right about that but panicking wouldn't do any of them any good. In an attempt to seem as if she wasn't worried, Marli climbed down from the ladder she was standing on and said, "Let go, Bridge, let me set these over the dining room table and chairs so they don't get wrinkled."

"I'll do that—you let him in," Bridget said, obviously fearing another scene. Then more sternly to Holt as she passed him she said, "And you—don't make things worse!"

Dalton was coming up the porch steps by then and had nearly reached the front door.

A glance at Holt told Marli that her brother's demeanor had changed from good-humoredly impatient to stiff, angry marine again. She doubted her sister-in-law's warning would help.

"Bridget's right," she told her brother.

But Holt didn't respond, he just stared at the front door as Dalton's knock sounded.

Marli wanted to call a simple *come in* as if they were all friends. But, sensing that wasn't a good idea, she went to the door and opened it.

"Hi," she said, making an attempt to sound as if she wasn't fearing the worst.

"I need to see Holt," Dalton said. Thankfully, this time it sounded like a statement of fact rather than the hostile demand he'd leveled the first time he'd come here.

But the less contentious tone didn't alleviate any of Marli's stress over the very real possibility that he'd reached a decision about Holt's future. "He's right here…come in," she invited, wishing Dalton would give her any indication that she didn't have to worry, that anything at all about this was friendly.

But it was obvious that whatever had been happening between the two of them was suspended for the time being. This visit was solely marine business.

"What?" Holt called snidely as Dalton stepped over the threshold. "No MPs to escort me away to a brig somewhere? I'll bet I should at least sit at attention for this, though, shouldn't I? *Sir.*"

"How about you just shut that big mouth of yours and listen for once?" Dalton said as he went to face him.

"Please, Holt!" Bridget said with some heat in her own voice as she returned to the living room and sat on the coffee table beside her husband.

"It doesn't matter what I say, honey," he told her with a flip-of-a-switch change that turned his tone kind, gentle, loving. He looked over at her, gave her a small smile and took her hand as if to give her strength—or maybe draw on her strength for himself. "Look at his face, he's made up his mind," he said—and indeed, that did seem apparent.

"Then just hear him out," Marli interjected.

Holt's head pivoted slowly back to Dalton. He didn't say a word but somehow there was insolence even in his stare.

Dalton held his ground and the two men locked eyes.

Without any preamble, Dalton said, "I'm giving you an LOR—"

"What's that?" Bridget asked.

Holt answered flatly, "A letter of reprimand."

Dalton went on. "I'm taking no other action against you. The reprimand will come with a three month loss of pay but no reduction in grade, you'll be given an honorable medical discharge and retain all benefits—"

"Oh, thank God!" Bridget blurted out. Then, to Dalton, she added, "Thank you!" at the same moment Marli, too, breathed a sigh of relief and said a soft thank you of her own.

Neither man reacted. Not even their gazes wavered from that stare-down with each other.

"I'm doing this for one reason and one reason only," Dalton continued. "I've gone over your service record and—hard as it is for me to believe—you've served with distinction in all other ways, on all assignments. This will be on your record but that's it. There won't be any ramifications other than the pay."

"But you just couldn't resist it costing me something, and putting a black mark on my record," Holt sneered.

Bridget shot to her feet, angrily hurling Holt's hand back to him. "Stop it!" she shouted at her husband. "Just stop it! I don't care what happened between your families when you two were nothing but little boys—it doesn't matter anymore. You *know* what you did on that stupid mission was wrong, that it was a mistake. And you also know that the colonel and the senator want you locked up for it! This guy is risking his own career by going against their wishes to do anything less than that. He's going against them *for you*! You said that if you get out of this you want us to start thinking about having a baby—well I'm not having kids with someone who can't admit when he's screwed up! Who can't say thank you to someone who's going out on a limb for him! So say it! Say you were wrong! Say thank you!"

Stunned by this outburst from the always loving and supportive Bridget she knew, Marli's gaze went from her sister-in-law to her brother.

Holt was rigid and patently displeased.

Again he turned his head to Dalton and Marli held her breath, knowing how impossible it was for her brother to give any ground to Dalton.

"I was wrong," Holt said begrudgingly, in a clipped, stilted, forced voice. "And you could have taken everything I've worked for away. But you didn't. So thank you."

Marli looked to Dalton and still didn't breathe, uncertain what his response would be.

He could have shown some amusement or satisfaction from Holt buckling under an outburst from his wife. He could have rubbed it in. But he didn't. Instead, in much the same clipped, stilted, forced way, he said, "You're welcome."

Then he turned and walked out of the house.

And Marli finally took a breath. She echoed Bridget's *thank God* and followed Dalton out into the yard once more to also parrot her sister-in-law with another, "Thank you!"

"You don't owe me any thanks," Dalton said when he turned to her, the marine in him abating and the Dalton he'd come to be to her again reemerging. "I meant what I said—I based my decision *only* on his record. He's served well for as long as I have—I couldn't discount that even if he is a pain in my ass. It earned him one almost-free pass."

"I'm still grateful."

"Don't be—I was on the verge of court-martialing him until I went through his file. That really was the deciding factor. Not even that would have helped him if the girls we were sent to rescue had been injured or killed, but they're home safe and sound and unhurt. So I was forced to admit to myself that, given a record like his, I wouldn't have court-martialed any other decorated marine, either."

She believed him. But still, knowing how much guff her brother had given him over the years—and how heavily that grudge had factored into Holt's disastrous choices on the mission—he got credit for taking the high road.

"Will you be in trouble for this?"

Dalton laughed slightly. "I called the colonel before I came over here, gave him my decision. He was pretty hot under the collar, so we'll have to wait and see how it plays out. But we've been on otherwise good terms before this so hopefully he'll cool off and not look for payback."

"And the senator?"

"I'm sure his nose will be bent out of shape, too—I doubt he'll ask me to be his next aide," Dalton joked. "But I'll go back to my unit, there'll be another assignment, another job, another mission, and it'll all blow over."

He'll go back...

Marli was so relieved for her brother and Bridget, so grateful to Dalton and impressed by him, that she hadn't thought beyond this. Until he said that.

"You were sent here to make this decision—and now that you've done it, you'll leave..." she muttered more to herself than to him.

"But not tonight," Dalton said. "Remember we saw the signs around town the other night, tonight the whole town is celebrating the formal launch of Micah's brewery and his full line of beers. The festival is just for him. How about we go?"

That helped blunt the sudden realization that their time together was coming to an end. Not much, but some.

"Okay," she said.

"Quinn, Tanner, Big Ben and I have to help Micah get enough beer into town first so I'll pick you up about eight?"

"Okay," she repeated.

"I'm due at the brewery to help load up. I have to get going. I'll see you then?"

"You will," she answered, staying where she was as he gave her a small wave and went down the drive.

Then she turned back to the house.

But her elation over her brother's reprieve was dampened.

And she knew why.

It was the reality that Dalton's time here would now come to an end.

After Dalton's announcement, hanging the living room drapes was forgotten about. Bridget's anger persisted and while Marli sided with her sister-in-law, Holt's continuing stubbornness caused a fight that escalated until Marli decided it would be best to leave them to it. She slipped out of the main house and headed for her shower.

It had been two hours since Dalton's visit to deliver his decision and she was still a little dazed. After months of worry over not only Holt's health but also over the potential consequences for his actions, it seemed too good to be true that he was in the clear, that she didn't need to worry anymore. There was an odd mix of relief and fear of letting go of that worry, as if without her bracing for disaster, something might go haywire.

Adding to that the realization that now Dalton would abruptly ride off into the sunset and it was as if she'd been spun around until she was too dizzy to see straight.

So she lingered in the shower, letting the water rain down on her for longer than usual, hoping that might help clear her head.

It did help wash away some of the frustration from dealing with Holt, but accepting that her brother was out of the woods only opened up an even larger soft spot for Dalton.

Yes, she was grateful to him but that was the smallest part of it. The greater part was what it told her about the man he was.

He could have nailed Holt to the wall and would have been well within his rights.

He could have buckled under pressure from higher-ups—and likely have helped his own promotion-path in the process.

He could have struck such a blow against Holt that it would have wiped out Holt's own stellar record of service and made it all for nothing.

He could have had the last laugh over Holt, the last word, the final blow, and it would have been no more than Holt deserved for nearly a lifetime of Holt taking a petty, childish grudge to extremes.

But Dalton hadn't done any of that. He'd potentially sacrificed himself for someone he didn't even like. He hadn't allowed his own well-earned anti-Holt feelings to rule. And to Marli that made him a very big man. A very big man who had stood there today and taken more of Holt's bad attitude as he'd delivered the decision that Holt should have bowed in gratitude for.

"You really made something of yourself, Mr. Camden," she said in awe of him as she finally got out of the shower.

"And now you'll leave…" she whispered.

She'd thought about so many things since discovering that Dalton had come to their small hometown. About him and their past. About the threat he posed to her brother. About what she should and shouldn't say and do and feel.

But she hadn't truly thought about him leaving. Not as things had blossomed and begun to grow between them. Not even last night, when she'd wanted to take him to her bed and he'd squashed that idea before she could broach it, when he'd warned her to be fully aware that it would be an only-for-now thing. But despite that warning she'd been stuck in should-she-or-shouldn't-she, without going beyond that.

Now the future beyond Dalton's decision had become real and looming. And that made it necessary for her to look before she leaped.

Of all the things she'd done without looking first, making love had never been one of them. She'd never had a one night stand. She had to have a relationship, feelings, a sense of closeness to someone before she'd ever been able to take that particular leap. And she'd never done it without believing there would be a tomorrow for them as a couple.

Now, with Dalton, she knew for a fact that there wouldn't be. He'd *told* her that there wouldn't be.

As she used a round brush to put waves into her hair as she dried it she reminded herself of all he'd told her—that being a marine came first and foremost for him, that his personal life took a backseat in his priorities, that sex and companionship were solely and completely recreational and only when he could fit them in to his schedule, in whatever part of the world he was in at the time, with whoever he could drum up.

If any other man on earth had said that to her she'd have walked away.

So do that...

But in spite of what her brain told her, her body said, *wait a minute...*

His image popped into her mind—tall and strong and muscular. His face a masterpiece.

She could hear his voice—deep and masculine.

She could feel once more what it was like to have him kiss her, touch her—things she wanted again. She wanted him to take her to the limit so badly she wasn't quite sure how to deal with it.

And she didn't know how she could walk away from any of it.

But if she didn't, if she answered the demand her

body was making, was she just asking to have her heart broken?

Or was she overreacting, making it a bigger deal than it was? It was undeniable that she'd broken her own heart when she'd left him seventeen years ago, but they'd been joined at the hip for nine years by then, they'd been as involved with each other as they could possibly have been. So of course it had hurt to have that end.

But now? They weren't *involved*. Their day-to-day existence wasn't intertwined, she noted as she applied careful, discreet makeup that would look natural while accentuating her eyes, her cheekbones, her lips.

This had been a reunion that had taken them from Dalton being furious with her to becoming friends again and even to rekindling a physical relationship, though that hadn't yet gotten very far. Surely that didn't constitute the kind of involvement that put hearts at risk.

This had just been an unexpected blip in her move home. He would leave—tomorrow or the next day or the next—and the blip would pass, her new life here in Merritt would carry on.

There wouldn't be a gap left by his absence, she thought as she put on the sundress she'd vetoed the night before. Patterns and habits hadn't been established. They weren't relying on each other. They weren't intrinsic parts of each other's lives. This time the stage was not set for hearts to be broken.

So what are you going to do? she asked herself as she slipped her feet into sandals and took a final look at herself in the mirror.

Her hair was in long fluffy waves around her shoulders. Her makeup was subtle but still highlighted her best features. Her dress was a flowy, lined white lace spaghetti-strap with a fairly-plunging V-neck that hinted at the cleavage her strapless bra created.

"Well, nothing about that says no, Marli."

Or that the effort she'd just put into it was going to lead her to walk away.

"But he's going to leave…" she reminded herself again, her voice ominous. "Don't forget that."

Much as she wished she might be able to, she didn't think she could.

She just wasn't sure what carried more weight— knowing he would leave or the weakness she'd realized so many days ago that she had for him.

The weakness she'd thought she could resist.

And so far hadn't been able to…

Merritt's town square had been turned over to the festival that was being called Camden Brewfest. In all honesty, it felt more like a giant wedding reception than anything.

Along the edges of the square were long tables. The first few offered all varieties of Camden beer, followed by tables and tables of potluck food, beginning with salads with beer-inspired dressings, moving on to chilis and ribs and all manner of main dishes and side dishes also featuring beer as an ingredient. Lastly came desserts from the local bakery that was now owned by Micah's fiancée, Lexie Parker, who had either incorporated the brews into her delicacies or offered suggestions for what beers and pastries paired.

Inside that table-formed perimeter was an abundance of dining tables and chairs that surrounded a portable dance floor and a platform for a popular band from the honky-tonk.

There were pearly colored balloons and congratulations banners along with T-shirts available to buy that touted the beer and the brewery. And as always, with any community gathering, there was a high turnout for the event.

Marli had been surprised to find Dalton's grandfather in the truck when Dalton picked her up. The elderly man's need for a ride into town had put her between him and his grandson, and the periodic brush of her arm against Dalton's kept her awareness of Dalton high. But Ben Camden chatted easily on the drive and she tried to fight that awareness by concentrating on what the older man had to say.

No sooner had Dalton parked near the library than Ben said, "Have a good time, kids," and got out to head toward the celebration.

"I think he has plans to meet up with some woman," Dalton confided at the slam of the passenger door once his grandfather had departed.

"Who?"

"I don't know but I heard him on the phone with someone named Harriet."

"Doesn't ring a bell," Marli said. "But good for him if he has a girlfriend."

Dalton laughed as he opened the driver's side door to get out then reached a hand back in for Marli.

Ohhh...she mentally lamented, knowing what placing her hand in his would do to her.

But she couldn't turn it down. As she knew it would, a tingling warmth seeped in the minute their hands met and climbed up her arm from there.

She worked to hide any evidence of it as she got out of the truck, too.

She couldn't help enjoying the way that Dalton was taking in the sight of her. When her feet hit the ground, he said, "You look like a million bucks tonight."

"So do you," she countered because it was true. Dalton managed to be a head-turner in just jeans and a dark blue Henley shirt with long sleeves pushed to muscled mid-forearms. And that slightly tousled head of coarse dark hair and his groomed scruff of beard only added to his sexiness.

He raised their clasped hands then, nodding to

them. "I don't suppose we should be seen like this or it'll cause talk."

"True," she agreed, loathe to let go but doing it simultaneously with him anyway, knowing it was for the best all the way around.

They headed across the church parking lot, making their way to the first table where Micah was the man of the hour. He was fielding rounds of compliments, felicitations and pats on the back from various well-wishers as they approached.

"Look at that," Dalton marveled proudly, "you forget just how much this town is one big family."

"Supporting their own, in your corner when it counts," Marli contributed. "You don't realize how special something like that is until you don't have it."

After offering their own hellos and kudos to Micah, and choosing the beers that appealed to each of them, they followed the line of attendees along the food tables. Once their dinner plates were full they joined Quinn, Tanner and their fiancées to eat.

Things between Marli and Dalton had still been tense the last time she'd seen the other Camden brothers—on the day when all four of them had helped with the remodel—and that had been reflected in Micah, Quinn and Tanner's response to her. They'd kept their distance. But as soon as they picked up on the fact that the tone between Marli and Dalton had changed, so did his brothers' attitude toward her. Tonight—like in years gone by when she and Dalton had been inseparable—they took her presence with them in stride and included her as if she was an accepted member of their ranks.

While they all ate they discussed who Harriet might be and where the mystery woman and their grandfather were. Since Ben had made no arrangements with any of them for a ride home, there was also a good bit of speculation about how he planned to get back to the farm or where he intended to spend the night.

The mayor took the stage as they were finishing eating to formally congratulate the newest enterprise in Merritt—the Camden Brewery. He encouraged loyalty to all local businesses and made a few jokes about the trouble-making Camden brothers coming home for three of the four to roost and take root again.

He ended by assuring them they were an asset to the community and welcomed them home before introducing the band. Then music and dancing began with gusto, catching most of the crowd up in the fun and drawing nearly everyone onto the floor—Marli and Dalton included.

While it might have been socially sanctioned physical contact, dancing with Dalton still had a potent effect on Marli. She knew she should opt out for her own peace of mind, but she was enjoying it too much to put an end to it. That resulted in dancing well into the night before she finally forced herself to claim she was dying for dessert to put an end to it.

Dessert for Dalton was a spicey cake that used some of his brother's citrus beer, and for Marli a triple-decker brownie with a stout ganache between the layers. As they'd often done at events like this in the past, they took their plates to the far sidelines where they sat together on top of a picnic table—feet on the bench seat—at a distance from everyone else. It left them close enough to the action to observe but at enough of a distance to be alone.

"This old place is something," Dalton said once they'd tasted and approved of their dessert choices. "I forgot how much fun it can be."

"Actually I didn't forget but over the years I wondered if it was as much fun as I remembered or if I'd built it up better in my mind."

"And the verdict?"

"It really is as fun as I thought. It's kind of infectious how everybody gets in there and has a good time."

"Have you visited much over the years?" Dalton asked.

"Once a long time ago when Bill Thompson retired and we needed someone new to oversee renting the house, then not again until I decided to move back. How about you?"

"Only twice in seventeen years. It's a subject I'm in trouble over with my family whenever it comes up."

"And I can see why! I didn't have any family or anyone else here to see—but you had your grandfather," she admonished.

"And that's the reason the subject gets me into trouble. I saw him more than twice—I flew him to meet me in various places where I was stationed, spent time with him that way, but here? Only the two times."

"Was it that hard for you to get back?"

"It was that hard for me to *be* back," he said candidly. "Every corner of this place reminded me of you and that was a sore spot. Splitting up the way we did cast a different light on all those years together and I started to think maybe I'd let you lead me around by the nose—"

"I did not!" Marli contended. "We were equal partners in crime."

"Yeah, I can see that again now. But when I was casting you as the evil villainess, everything to do with you was evil, too, so I repainted the picture in my mind, I guess."

He didn't say that with any malice so she didn't take it to heart and instead made light of it. "And you painted yourself as my innocent victim? I lured you and your ladder to my big bad tree when I was seven in a plot to make you my minion and do my bidding until I left you high and dry?"

"That was pretty much it, yeah," he confirmed.

"But now I'm not evil anymore?"

"Well…" he said with a crooked, intrigued half-smile, "Maybe a little wicked here and there but only in a fun way…"

She shoulder-chucked him and he stole the last bite of her brownie to punish her.

"Quite a change from then to now. Rather than it being hard to be here it's going to be hard to leave," he said then.

There it was once again—the reality that he would be gone soon.

It took Marli a moment to fully accept it. "When is that going to happen?"

"I have to make travel arrangements but likely in the next day or two."

She nodded. "The tables have turned and now you'll be the one of us taking off."

"It's not a payback, just what has to happen in the normal course of things," he said.

"I know," she said quietly as it sank in all the more that this unplanned reunion was coming to an end.

There *was* one thing she could do, though…

Dalton stood and took their plates and forks to a nearby trash can and her eyes went along, appreciating the view of his backside and weathering a wave of desire that reminded her of how the previous evening had nearly ended.

Had he not cut things short she would have taken him to her bedroom for a night she didn't think either one of them would ever have forgotten. And he hadn't cut things short because he hadn't been willing, he'd done it to make sure she knew where they stood, to be clear that he would ultimately leave.

Now that was all too clear.

But was she going to just have him take her home now that him leaving was on the horizon? Was she going to say goodnight, wish him a safe trip to wherever, tell him to have a nice life?

She could. And she could do it with her conscience finally clear of the guilt that had trailed her since she'd left him behind, knowing she'd explained, apologized, and been forgiven.

She knew that was probably the best route—to part with him with the slate finally clean and no messy complications getting in their way. After all, doing anything else would be an only-for-now thing, and she might regret it.

Or she might not…

She thought about that.

Rarely in her life had she regretted taking a chance, going where she hadn't been before, having a new experience—even if she knew it had a limited lifespan.

What she *had* regretted were the few occasions when she *hadn't* taken the chance, when she hadn't let herself have the experience.

And suddenly she knew that would be the case here—if she didn't take the leap that her whole body, her whole being had been wanting to take with Dalton, she would regret it.

Her weakness for him was just stronger than any reason to deny herself.

He returned to the picnic table and held out his hand the way he had to help her out of his truck earlier. "Back to dancing?"

Marli looked up into his blue eyes and shook her head. But she did take his hand. "I don't think we should waste what time we have left."

There was a sultriness to her tone that told him all he needed to know about how she wanted to put that time to use. His eyebrows arched as a knowing smile erupted on his supple mouth. "And that's my Marli," he said, enveloping her hand to take her to his truck.

The drive home was silent but the air was charged between them—like it had been on many teenage drives to park at the local make-out spot on Potter's Point. But tonight it was her place they went to, her bedroom she led him to exactly as she'd wanted and imagined doing Friday night.

"I'd ask you if you're sure," he said in a gruff voice when they reached the moonlit foot of her bed and she turned into his arms, "but I know once you've made up your mind—"

"I'm sure," she confirmed anyway. "But you don't have to if you don't want to," she challenged—something she'd done often at the start of an escapade, knowing that it would just spur him on.

His grin was lazy and so, so sexy. "Oh, I want to…" he confirmed, locking his arms around her, low on the small of her back before he returned the challenge in brief, taunting, hit-and-run kisses that kicked off a playfulness between them until one lingered, softer, sweeter, and with a simmering sensuality.

Marli settled into that kiss with a bit of coyness to start but kissing him was too wonderful not to captivate her quickly. Her lips parted to match his and when his tongue made its entrance she greeted it, sending her hands up the wall of his chest to his neck and into his hair.

A rush of dizzying sensations took all of her focus as Dalton lowered the zipper down her spine and let his big hands splay against her back.

His T-shirt was tucked into his jeans and she pulled the tails free so she could do the same, eager for the sleek warmth of his skin. Sleek and warm and rock-hard, she explored every expanse, every dip, every mound that made up that masterpiece of muscles and sinews.

Getting her fill of that, though, his shirt began to seem more and more in her way so she interrupted their kiss briefly to pull it off over his head.

He used that interruption to flick her shoulder with the tip of his tongue while he slid both lace straps of her sundress down her arms, spreading the V-neck wide and low on the upper swells of breasts that had been contained only by the shelf of bra that lined the bodice. Then he went lower and kissed that upper swell of one breast, setting off little sparks in her and turning her nipples taut with anticipation.

Anticipation he left unappeased by returning to her mouth again once his shirt was off, kissing her with a new intimacy.

Having his torso bare helped distract her from those awakening yearnings and she let her hands travel over it all—front and back, her palms learning the honed contours of pecs that he hadn't had years ago.

There was nothing boyish left in the man and those broad shoulders, those solid biceps, the pure breadth of his back proved it.

As they went on kissing she began to have the sense that there was something different for her in this. Different from the one and only love-making event that had clumsily disposed of their virginities. But also different from any other time for her with other partners, too—even with the men she had once thought she would marry. This was better. More natural and organic. It just felt right in a way that nothing had for her yet and it drew her in further than she'd ever been, allowing her to give herself completely over to it, to him. So completely that when his index fingers hooked the straps of her dress where they languished on her upper arms and pulled them down so her dress could fall around her feet, she was not only unshy about that loss of clothing but glad for it, adding to it by easing out of her sandals, too.

That dropped her inches lower but Dalton compensated for it, his massive body curving around her like a cocoon that sheltered her body, now clad in nothing more than scant lace bikini briefs.

He stepped out of his own shoes and shoved them aside but that didn't change his height, it just seemed to give her license to find the bulging zipper of his jeans and lower it.

She took his guttural groan as encouragement and finished the task, pushing his jeans and what was beneath them far enough off his hips to drop to the ground, allowing him to step out of them.

He was naked now and she wanted to see him.

She broke away from that kiss and leaned backward to take in the sight.

More impressive than anything she'd expected, she drank in the view, letting admiring hands course over his chest, his flat abs, and downward to narrow hips that framed massive evidence of how much he wanted her.

He didn't indulge her study of him for long. His arms tightened and he swung her around, picked her up as if she weighed nothing and deposited her onto her bed.

He took a turn at getting his own eyeful of her, his handsome face showing admiration and a hunger for what he saw before he retrieved something from the front pocket of his jeans and joined her.

His lean, taut body half-covered hers and he recaptured her mouth in another ravishing kiss while he laid a palm to her stomach and then coursed upward until he found breasts starving for his attention.

There was no question that he had a magic touch. When he switched from one breast to the other and abandoned their kissing to take that first one into the dark velvet of his mouth, delight arched her spine and robbed her of all inhibition, all thought but the wonders of his flicking, tracing, teasing tongue, and his tenderly nipping, tormenting teeth.

She angled just enough to reach a hand to that shaft of steel waiting for her, feeling Dalton's whole body stiffen with pleasure at her first touch.

What little restraint either of them had was quickly shed. Hands and mouths aroused, bodies writhed, and need welled up until it demanded satisfaction.

With little effort or time wasted Dalton applied the condom then pressed her to lie flat so that he could position himself over her, fitting perfectly between her thighs to find a welcoming home inside of her. It took nothing for them to discover their own unique rhythm, to move in unison in a way that brought him deeper and deeper into her, that drove them both to a fevered pitch. It wasn't long until an unequaled, explosive climax caught Marli in its grip, washing over her in wave after wave of a bliss so exquisite she could only cling fiercely to him, wanting never to come out of it.

She knew her nails were digging into his back but she couldn't help it and he must not have been bothered by it because as she began to ease from her own peak she felt his magnificent body tense as he plunged even deeper into her and froze with a culmination of his own that was so intense she felt it ripple through him.

And then everything came slowly to a stop, leaving them both utterly spent.

Dalton insinuated his hands beneath her and rolled to his back, taking her to lie on top of him, their bodies still wonderfully united, his chest an impeccable pillow for her head, his arms tight around her to keep her melded to him.

"I got kind of lost…" he said in a gravelly voice then. "I didn't hurt you, did I?"

"No, but I think I might have hurt you—"

He laughed. "I didn't feel any pain…"

"I may have left marks on your back," she persisted.

"Oh, yeah…" he said, as if he had only just realized. "I'll probably survive but if you give me a little break we can see if I'm any the worse for wear…" He flexed inside of her to make his intention obvious. "What do you say?"

"I'd say we'd better test you out, just in case," she

played along, thinking that she could happily stay just the way she was forever.

She didn't have that opportunity because he rolled them again and left her on her side while he disappeared into her bathroom for a scant minute before returning to reposition them once again—him on his back once more, her pulled so close to his side that there wasn't even air between them.

Then he reached for her thigh to bring it over his, clamped his arms firmly around her again as if he wanted them sealed to each other, and settled his chin atop her head where it rested on his chest once more.

"We were always good together but that topped everything," he whispered then.

"Everything…" Marli agreed just as quietly before replete exhaustion overwhelmed her and freed her from thinking about how this night with him was ultimately destined to end.

Chapter Nine

"Three weddings, christening Tanner's baby and Pops here getting a lifetime achievement award for his volunteering—complete with a big-deal, fancy-formal gala in Billings to honor him. Any chance you'll be around for some of that?" Micah asked Dalton at brunch on Sunday.

Dalton had barely made it home for the brunch. Leaving Marli's bed had *not* held much appeal for him after their night together. Not at all. But his grandfather had invited everyone as the last opportunity for the whole family to be together before Dalton left again, and once Dalton was with them that had been great, too.

Not as great as being with Marli but great enough to strike a chord in him. Especially after all the talk of weddings and the christening and the award his grandfather had just been notified of—all events that he would be sad to miss.

"You know the answer to that as well as I do," Dalton said. "There's no telling where I'll be or if I can get away. And since I just got word that my unit is being sent to Eastern Europe—"

"There's not much of any chance," Ben concluded for him, his tone gloomy and concerned.

The new female members of the family had left to meet various other obligations and only the brothers and their grandfather remained. But Micah, Quinn and Tanner had been there another hour since their significant-others had taken off and had now said they should get going as well, bringing the brunch to a conclusion.

"What I will do," Dalton announced, getting up from the dining room table and gathering what hadn't already been cleared, "is the dishes."

There was no argument or insistence on helping but Quinn said, "You'll make the rounds to say good-bye before you leave, right?"

"Sure," Dalton said, taking the last of the coffee mugs and a heavy feeling with him to the kitchen.

His grandfather had made a feast of food for brunch and he'd indulged in plenty of it, but the heavy feeling didn't have anything to do with what he'd eaten. It went deeper than that.

Deconstructing it as he rinsed dishes he thought

about how his goal for the last seventeen years had been to steer clear of Merritt and the memories it held for him. Having been legitimately kept away by his career had really just helped him accomplish that personal goal. Crossing paths with his brothers in the course of his service and theirs, having his grandfather come to him rather than him going to Ben had satisfied him when it came to family and visits. But things had somehow changed through the course of this trip and he discovered he wasn't thrilled with the looming need to leave Merritt or his family.

The big turning point was overcoming his anger at Marli. That had freed him enough to enjoy being in Merritt again. Truth be told, he'd more than enjoyed it, he'd gained a new appreciation for the small town. A fresh perspective. He'd come to see the small town through the eyes of a well-traveled adult who had witnessed and experienced enough to recognize how nice it could be to live a more peaceful, simple life in a place where—for the most part—people knew each other, cared about each other, looked out for, helped and celebrated each other. This small town where he'd had his start had a lot to offer. There were lots of places and occasions where it had felt good to be included again. The way Micah, Quinn and Tanner would be from here on out.

He was a little jealous of that.

But he wasn't only jealous of his brothers being back in Merritt. He was also jealous of the time they would have together, the opportunity to be integral parts of each others' lives from now on, to be in those weddings, go to those christenings, and have these last years with Ben, too. While he wouldn't.

It bothered him. It bothered the hell out of him. It made him feel something he hadn't felt before— it made him feel like an outsider in his own family.

Having filled the dishwasher, he closed and started it, then turned to cleaning the counters and the stovetop. He reminded himself that in order for his brothers to have what they would now have, they'd put their careers in the marines behind them.

That was no small thing.

And yet, when he thought about it, he still recognized in himself a greater desire for their new lives than for returning to his. He found himself wanting what they'd found here with the women who had returned to their lives.

The women…

He huffed slightly at himself, at what he was only slinking up to in his own mind—Marli.

His desire for Marli was greater than his desire to go back to the marines, to his life of the last seventeen years, to anything that didn't include her.

What he had a greater desire for was to go across the street, back to Marli so that they could share more time together, exploring and enjoying each other like they had in bed and out of it.

Because another change that had happened on this trip was in where things stood between them.

"And that's really what this is about," he muttered under his breath, understanding suddenly that while some of this heavy feeling was based in what he would miss with his family, a much bigger portion of it was the idea of leaving Marli.

He stopped wiping off the kitchen table and instead leaned over it, both hands flat to the surface, his head hanging between his shoulders, giving in to what was actually going on with him.

It had been good to be with her again. Better than he could ever have imagined. Even with the stress of deciding what to do about Holt they'd still managed to resolve their old issues and reconnect. They'd even managed to reach another level in being together.

And he didn't want to let that go.

He didn't want to let *her* go…

He'd meant it when he'd told her that everything with him was fine because it had been. R and R hookups, no-strings-attached fun to regroup and decompress, nothing deep or serious—that had been all he'd needed or wanted from and with any of the other women he'd known.

But now nothing seemed fine about leaving Marli. At this point, he couldn't imagine returning to just those R and R hookups. They would never be able to satisfy him again. Not when he'd been reminded of what it was like to sincerely connect with someone…with Marli. To have the to-the-core, adult feelings for her that put those ancient childhood-born ones to shame. That made it impossible to return to nothing-but-fun hookups. Those hookups that Marli had been right about—they had been safe because he hadn't cared.

But now there was no denying that he cared about Marli again.

And thinking about being without her again rattled him. He wanted to be with her, to have a future with her, kids with her.

Like his brothers would have with the women they'd chosen.

Because that was what he wanted, too…

Years ago Marli had been everything to him but they'd been too young, too naive, too inexperienced to make their relationship work. They'd needed to grow beyond it, to go their separate ways, learn who they were on their own, without the influence or safety net of the twosome. But this time with her had reminded him of what she'd been to him. Their rare and unique friendship had reformed, and they had managed to forge something new on top of it. Something that felt like a stronger, rooted connection that was better than before.

So much better that he couldn't accept even the thought of *dis*connecting now. Not even for the marines.

He'd told her that if he ever started to feel like he

was missing out on anything he'd change course. Well, here it was—leaving Merritt made him feel like he would be missing out on what life could be like living permanently in his old hometown. Leaving his brothers and his grandfather made him feel like he would be missing out on the day-to-day and the milestones of the family he had and what was left of his grandfather's life.

But more importantly, leaving Marli made him feel like he would be missing out on his own life, on having a life with her.

And it struck him suddenly and hard that he *did* want a change of course if that change of course could include her. That without her he could very well feel like life had passed him by. That life without her would be half a life.

His grandfather had said that he'd never seen two people who belonged together more than the two of them, and as everything settled over him, Dalton believed that was true.

At least he knew it was true for him.

Was it true for Marli?

She *had* left him in her dust seventeen years ago…

And she was three-for-three in bailing on futures with other guys…

And it would kill him to find out that ending things with him after the miscarriage had been a once-and-for-all for her despite their current reunion.

But it was possible, he admitted to himself. It was possible she would break his heart all over again...

But suddenly there was too much at stake for him *not* to take the chance.

"I saw Camden come out of your place this morning," her brother greeted her when he saw Marli on Sunday afternoon.

"Mind your own business, Holt," Bridget warned her husband.

Bridget had called to say the fight Marli had slipped away from the day before was over—if not resolved—and asked her to come to the main house so they could make another attempt to hang the living room drapes.

Marli had assured her sister-in-law that she would be there, but it had taken her some time to get herself to shower and dress even in simple jeans and two layers of T-shirts—a white tee under a blue U-neck. She'd shampooed her hair but hadn't had the oomph to do anything more than allow it to air-dry before she'd just brushed it and left it loose. Then—in answer to the overwhelming blues that had her in their grip—she'd landed on a chair at her kitchen table when she'd meant to walk out the door toward the main house.

After over an hour of sitting there, crying and feeling miserable at the knowledge that this short time she'd had with Dalton was finished, she'd worked to get herself under control.

By then she'd had to hold a cold, wet washcloth to her eyes to hide the telltale evidence of her tears before she could make good on her promise to Bridget. She'd finally managed to cross the backyard but now that she was with Holt and Bridget in the kitchen of her childhood home she wasn't up to dealing with her brother's attitude toward Dalton. She appreciated her sister-in-law's intervention.

Unfortunately Holt ignored his wife's advice and said, "I hope it was just a last hurrah and now he'll get the hell out of town and stay out."

Dalton hadn't been gone half an hour before he'd texted her that he was being sent overseas. That had only made her feel worse and the second text saying he would come to say goodbye before he left hadn't helped. Holt's words rubbed salt into the wound.

"I imagine he's packing as we speak—he and his unit have new orders," she said, fighting not to break down again.

"Good!" Holt said with brash satisfaction that Marli had trouble accepting.

"He did you a good turn, Holt," she said with a hint of anger.

It didn't faze her brother. "Don't let that buy him another shot with you. You were smart enough to get rid of him once before—"

"I didn't *get rid* of him. We needed to part ways so we could both grow up and do all the things we needed to do. I still cared about him." And she always had, despite it fading into the background until she'd set eyes on him again.

"You *cared* or *care*?" her brother challenged.

"Both," she said with weary honesty, knowing that old and new feelings for Dalton were only making losing him harder.

"Tell me that last night was just a booty call to the past and not that you've started something up with him again," Holt demanded.

"I'm not going to tell you anything because Bridget is right—it's none of your business."

Her brother didn't balk at that, either. "It's got nowhere to go if he's leaving town," he observed with clear satisfaction.

"Nothing is going anywhere," she said under her breath because it was true. It was something she'd had to force herself to recall again and again since Dalton had left her bed. After the night they'd had together, after making love multiple times, after lying so perfectly in his arms this morning, it had taken quite a bit for her to return to the real world where Dalton would be leaving soon. The real world where she had to look at him going as nothing more than two old friends parting again at the end of a successful reunion. The real world she'd gone into last night with her eyes wide open and with fair warning that that one night was all they were going to have.

"Just drop it, okay?" she beseeched her brother.

"Be grateful that you aren't being court-martialed, let go of that stupid grudge and let's move on."

Which was also what she'd been telling herself—that seeing Dalton again had been only a fortunate happenstance that had allowed her to mend fences with him. That now he would leave and she would go on as if he'd never been here. She would start her practice, help Bridget care for and acclimate Holt to his future, and they would all go on to the next stage of their lives. Rather than being sad over what she wouldn't have, she should be grateful that she would now be able to do that free of the guilt she'd carried around with her for seventeen years over the way she'd treated Dalton after the miscarriage.

But apparently urging Holt to change the subject just made him more bullheadedly determined to continue with it. "Keep those three broken engagements in mind. Remember that you and serious, permanent relationships don't mix—you said it yourself. Not to mention that Camden was the first one you nixed even before Nolan, Clint and Arnie. You wouldn't go back with any of them, why would you go back to the one who came before them? You don't want to be all tied up in a *we* and have to curb yourself because of it. You don't want to be Mom, you don't want the life Mom had as A Wife and nothing but A Wife. You want something else for yourself."

Listening to her brother made Marli wish she hadn't talked so much. But she couldn't deny what he was saying when she *had* said it herself. And meant it.

"Leave her alone, Holt," Bridget said sympathetically, as if she could see how despondent Marli already was.

"I won't leave her alone!" he brother exclaimed. "She put that guy in the rearview mirror when she was barely more than a kid, she can't fall back into something with him now! I already told Yancy to cool his heels, that she's dead set against getting together with another guy for now. I told him to give her time and space before he asks her out because she's swearing off men and relationships till she figures out why she's allergic to marriage and what she really wants, what suits her. I'm just making sure she doesn't lose sight of all that. I'm holding her to it so she doesn't make another damn mistake!"

"I haven't lost sight of anything," Marli said, trying to make sure she truly hadn't.

She understood where this was coming from with Holt—that he hated and had always hated her closeness with someone he considered his enemy. But he also wasn't wrong about what she'd gone through, and the boundaries she'd put in place to protect herself. She tried to use her brother's harsh reminders as he intended them—to keep her from missing the importance of her track record and the very real reasons she'd ended her engagements and opted to change course when it came to future relationships.

She honestly did need not to lose sight of the conclusion she'd come to that she might well need to find a less traditional path that might suit her better, to live her life on her own terms rather than expecting marriage in her future.

"Let's just hang the drapes, okay?" Bridget suggested.

"Yes! Please," Marli pleaded, taking the lead to go into the living room.

Bridget and Holt followed her but the change of scenery didn't stop her brother's rant.

"You counted Camden out once," he continued. "That means he already made you hit the panic button the same way the other three did. Don't think it won't happen again just because this is Act Two or something. He's still one of your rejects."

Bridget had gone to the picture window and after a gaze through it she said, "Well, this particular reject is coming up the drive."

To say goodbye…

That knowledge took more of the starch out of Marli and made her want to hide.

Not letting him say the words won't keep him here, she told herself.

Which was for the best. If he stayed around he could blind her to the risks she'd face in a relationship and potentially put her on the mistaken path she'd gone down three times before. The path that she'd learned was not right for her.

Saying nothing else to Bridget or Holt she went outside.

Dalton was wearing cammo pants and an army-green T-shirt that hugged those impressive muscles she'd had her hands all over last night and this morning.

That memory made her want to touch him again—but that would just make it harder to say goodbye, so she jammed both hands into her pockets, trying not to hunch her shoulders as she met him and said a feeble, "Hi."

"Hi yourself," he returned, sounding more resolute than she did. Not only did his clothes tell her he was ready to get back to being a marine, so did his tone.

It's for the best...

His eyes went to the house before he nodded in the direction he'd come from and said, "Walk with me?"

A glance over her shoulder told Marli that Holt and Bridget were both at the window. She didn't want an audience for this any more than Dalton did.

"Sure," she agreed, continuing on around him.

Dalton turned and fell into step with her as she headed away from those watching eyes.

Once they reached the road, it was natural to turn in the direction of *their* tree the way they always had. Neither of them said anything. Marli assumed Dalton was carefully choosing his words so she left him to it. Once they reached the enormous oak, she did something else she'd done often years ago—she rested her back against the trunk. With her hands still in her pockets she waited for him to get on with it.

"You know," he began then, standing a few feet in front of her and towering above her, "to get through you ditching me seventeen years ago I had to make myself believe I hated you."

It was no less than she'd earned from him—but she hadn't had any sleep, and she was feeling very vulnerable after the argument with her brother despite the truth in Holt's tough-love words. If Dalton needed to have some last airing of what a rotten thing she'd done, some last comeuppance, she wasn't sure she could take it.

"I know," she said in a voice barely above a whisper.

"But I don't think I ever really *did* hate you. Being with you again now made me realize how much I definitely *don't* hate you anymore even if I did. I am grateful that you went, that you left—not for the *way* you did it, but for your reasons, and the way you worked to put us both on the right paths."

"Okay…"

"It was what needed to happen," he continued. "And if you hadn't done it we might have stuck around here, I might not have ever gone to Annapolis, gotten my degree, become a marine. I'm proud of my service—"

"You should be."

"And you would have missed all the places you've been and the things you've done—all those experiences you wanted to have. If you hadn't had them you would never have been happy or content."

"No, I wouldn't have," she agreed, thinking that this wrap-up was a demonstration of a proper way to bring the time they'd had together to a conclusion, giving it the closure she hadn't allowed either of them before.

"So no hard feelings," she said to aid the conclusion.

"And now we can both really go on."

She nodded and blinked away the moisture that rushed to her eyes again. She took a deep breath, and opened her eyes wide to dry them out, to make certain she was seeing and thinking clearly, and said, "Promise me you'll do everything you can to stay safe."

He chuckled. "Oh, I don't think there's much danger I need to worry about."

What did that mean?

"I'm not leaving, Marli," he said then.

"You're not being sent overseas after all?"

"My unit is going, I'm just not going with them."

"You've been sent somewhere else?" she asked, still unsure what he was trying to tell her.

He shook his head. "Don't make a run for it when you hear this, but I'm not going anywhere. I'm gonna resign my commission."

"Because of Holt and the court-martial? Are the colonel and the senator drumming you out?"

Dalton shook his head. "Being here, with my family, with you, hashing through everything from before, has taken me to a place I never expected to find myself. It's brought up stuff in me that I didn't even know was there—"

He went on to talk about the merits of Merritt, about a sense of missing out if he left his family here and went back to business as usual himself, knowing that he'd be absent for so many important events for his family, about his discovery that he wanted to be a part of the next chapter in his brothers' lives.

"And it just hit me that I want the next chapter in my own life, too," he said.

Marli wasn't sure what, exactly, he was getting at and merely frowned at him.

"I meant it when I told you I was okay—happy—putting my career first, that I thought I *was* experiencing enough for me without giving much attention to the private side of my life. But being with my brothers, seeing where they're going, seeing them coupled-up, Tanner with a kid…and then hearing what you said about that stuff…it got me thinking in a way I just haven't before. In a way that made me wonder if you were right—that if I don't look beyond the marines, if I end up without that whole part of life ever taking shape…well, I started to wonder if I *would* regret it."

He sighed and shook his head before going on. "I think I've gone full-circle. What I need to do now—what I *want* to do now is come back to where I started. If I don't, I know that I'll be sorry. As sorry as we both would have been if we hadn't ever left in the first place. I told you if I ever started to feel like I'm missing out I'd do something about it, change course—but it's not happening someday, it's happening today and it hit me like a tank. So I'm doing something about it."

"Leaving the marines."

"And coming home to stay in Merritt." He paused, came a step nearer and said, "Hopefully with you… As a choice, not out of necessity or circumstances but because I want you, and I want to be with you."

It was a clear and simple statement but still enough to throw Marli off balance. She had to take her hands out of her pockets and grasp the sides of the tree to steady herself as a voice in her head that sounded suspiciously like her brother told her that if this was going where she thought it was going she couldn't let herself do what she'd done three times before. She couldn't let herself be swept up in the moment and lose sight of all the potential problems ahead. She couldn't dismiss things she knew, realizations she'd already come to when she was thinking straight, when she wasn't emotional, when she was calm and rational.

"Oh, Dalton…" she lamented, distressed at the

mere possibility of being in the position she thought she was about to be in.

His sexy mouth stretched into that slow, knowing smile that said he was reading her mind. "I'm not proposing to you."

"You're not?" she asked, confused by why that didn't bring relief, why it somehow didn't make her feel good at all.

"What kind of an idiot would I be to propose to somebody who freaks out at the idea of marriage?"

She couldn't argue with that. "So what *are* you saying?" she asked.

"I'm saying it's always been you, Marli. Ever since I found you up this tree. I didn't see it until it was too late but Bella was a way to prove something to myself, a late rebound. And after that…it wasn't that I didn't let anyone get close because it kept me safe, it was that they couldn't get close because they weren't you. Being with you again finally made me realize that."

He shrugged and repeated, "It's always been you and it will always *be* you. I want *you*. I don't care if it's in a way that fits the mold or a way we make up ourselves. I want a future with you in it every single day of the rest of my life. I want it here in Merritt. I want a family with you—kids—and I want it no matter what shape it has to take. If that means we live in separate houses the way we always have, okay. If that means we live together but never get married, okay. If that means we're some kind of weird, extended-special-friends, okay. I'll do whatever the hell it takes not to scare you, not to send you into your marriage panic, not to make you feel swallowed up or like you're in quicksand. I want you in whatever way it takes."

She didn't have a quick response because what he was saying gave her pause and made her think.

He didn't want her to feel the things she'd told him her other engagements had caused.

But she realized that Dalton had never made her feel any of those things.

The fear and panic that had sent her running seventeen years ago had come from the fact that the idea of staying in Merritt with him *had* appealed to her. It had come from being terrified that if she gave in to that appeal she might end up as unhappy as her mother had been.

The fear and panic in her last engagements had come from discovering that her fiancés wanted her to be different than she actually was. But that had never been the case with Dalton so it struck her that there was no reason for her to believe that would change. So, ultimately, there was no reason for her to panic.

She and Dalton had already been a *we* for years and years…

We should watch the fireworks from up high…

We should check out that cave…

We should try a cigarette…a beer…sex…

And not only had that *we* never bothered her, she'd liked having him as a partner, a cohort, a companion and conspirator. She'd liked sharing everything with him. It hadn't taken anything away from her and she hadn't even once felt as if she'd lost any of herself to it.

With Dalton, being a *we* had just meant she had someone she *could* rely on if she needed to. It had given her strength and extra courage. It had made nothing seem insurmountable.

She'd accepted three proposals because marriage—a marriage that was different than what her mother had had—*was* what she wanted. It was just that she'd come to feel that those relationships would have demanded things from her that would have made her unhappy, too.

But Dalton had been right when he'd said that was an issue of the men themselves. Dalton was a man different from the other three. So marriage to him would also be different. Different in that way she'd been looking for.

Thinking about marriage with him, about having kids with him, actually took away fear and panic, and made her feel *more* able to do those things. He empowered her now in just the same way that doing wild, adventurous things together when they were kids had boosted her courage.

But she needed these new realizations she was having to sink in—she wanted them to have a chance to settle a bit more before sharing them, even with him. Instead she said, "You're willing to change the whole course of your life so we can be friends?"

"I am," he said without hesitation. "I'm willing to leave the marines because I don't want just bits and pieces of this next chapter between missions and deployments and answering the call of duty. I want to dive in free of anything that could take me away from you again. And when it comes to us, we grew up doing things on our own terms—for better or worse—so why can't we do that again?"

He closed even more of the distance between them without crowding her. "I love you, Marli—that's the bottom line. Once upon a time it was puppy love, then it was teenage love, and now it's real, for-all-time, you're-all-I-want love. That means I'm okay doing whatever you need me to do to get us there. Because I know—and I think you do, too—that no two people have ever been better together than we are."

"I do know that," she whispered, admitting it aloud and also acknowledging to herself that what she'd rediscovered with him had been sorely lacking with all three of the other significant men in her past.

She also knew that Dalton *would* accept her in whatever way she needed him to because he always had. Not once had he ever expected her to be anything but herself with him, or tone herself down. Nothing about her had ever made him balk. He'd never condemned or found fault up until that last decision that had broken them apart. In fact, he'd celebrated her, joined in, supported and stood by her.

He'd set the standard for other men by accepting her as-is, and no one else could live up to it.

Or to the man he was.

A man with a strength that neither Nolan nor Clint nor Arnie had had in any measure, a strength that couldn't be intimidated by any controversy she stirred up. A strength that had always made him ready to catch her if she did take a misstep. And all without being somehow threatened if she *didn't* need him.

The kind of genuine strength that went beyond the physical powerhouse that stood before her and let him withstand pressure from a superior officer and a senator over Holt's court-martial—something that hadn't been easy and that had been more to his detriment than to his benefit. The kind of strength that even had him rising above Holt's bad behavior and attitude.

But what about Holt?

"You know my brother comes in the deal," she reminded. And maybe tested, too.

"Always did," Dalton said without skipping a beat. "I've dealt with him before, I can deal with him again. No matter what he does, it's worth it to me to be with you."

She'd just had a full taste of her brother's attempt to keep her away from Dalton and she knew Holt's grudge against him wasn't likely to ever make a life with Dalton smooth. But as all he was saying, as all she was thinking and feeling was settling in, so was the knowledge that Holt's antagonism didn't change anything for her if Dalton was okay with it. That weathering the worst Holt could dish out was worth it for her, too. That anything was worth whatever it took for her to be with this man who everything in her told her she was meant to be with.

Her grasp on the tree trunk let up and she cocked her chin at him. "But would you marry me if I asked you to?" she challenged.

"Are you testing the waters or proposing?" he countered.

She smiled smugly. "I'm proposing."

"As opposed to *accepting* a proposal? You think you doing the asking will make the difference?"

"I think *you* make the difference," she said without a doubt about any of it anymore. "You—and the fact that I love you like I've never loved anyone else. Being with you again now has shown me that. No one can compare to you and nothing comes anywhere close to what being with you means to me. What being with you has always meant to me. Being just friends with you in any form could never be enough."

"Then yes."

"To my proposal?"

"To your proposal and anything else you want—

the same as it ever was," he said, reaching for one of her arms and pulling her away from the tree and into his embrace. "But know that if you ever disappear on me again I'll track you to the ends of the earth—and now I know how to do it."

"I've been to the ends of the earth, now I just want to be here in plain old Merritt with you."

And she'd never meant anything more.

She wrapped her arms around the man who had grown from the boy who found her up a tree, and looked into those blue eyes she never wanted to be without again.

"I love you, Dalton," she told him seriously. "I want to spend the rest of my life with you no matter what. I want to live in the same house with you—"

"But not in your brother's backyard," Dalton interjected.

"And so it begins—already demanding compromises and sacrifices."

She was just joking but still he said, "The same kind of compromises and sacrifices we made to make sure we didn't kill ourselves jumping off the mill bridge into the river in our inner-tubes—equal partners. Who don't live in your brother's backyard," he reiterated.

"Definitely not in my brother's backyard," she confirmed. "And regardless of what Holt dishes out—because he definitely won't like this."

"Maybe he'll come around someday," Dalton suggested. "When he sees that there's nothing he can do now any more than there was anything he could do when we were kids to break us up. Maybe he'll give in for the sake of nieces or nephews or both that are his family, too."

"Maybe. But whether he does or not, what's important is that I never have to be without you again because that's one experience I don't want to repeat—once was enough."

He told her he loved her again and then gave her a kiss that brought them completely back to where they belonged.

To a new beginning for them that Marli knew was exactly where every road had been intended to lead—into each other's arms.

Now and forever more.

* * * * *

#2983 FORTUNE'S RUNAWAY BRIDE
The Fortunes of Texas: Hitting the Jackpot • by Allison Leigh
Isabel Banninger's fiancé is a two-timing jerk! Running out of her own wedding leads her straight into CEO Reeve Fortune's strong, very capable arms. Reeve is *so* not her type. But is he the perfect man to get this runaway bride to say "I do"?

#2984 SKYSCRAPERS TO GREENER PASTURES
Gallant Lake Stories • by Jo McNally
Web designer Olivia Carson hides her physical and emotional scars behind her isolated country life. Until a simple farmhouse remodel brings city-boy contractor Tony Vello crashing into her quiet world. They share similar past pain...and undeniable attraction. But will he stay once the job is done?

#2985 LOVE'S SECRET INGREDIENT
Love in the Valley • by Michele Dunaway
Nick Reilly adores Zoe Smith's famous chocolate chip cookies—and Zoe herself. He hides his billionaire status to get closer to the single mom. Even pretends to be her fiancé. But trading one fake identity for another is a recipe for disaster. Unless it saves Zoe's bakery *and* her guarded heart...

#2986 THE SOLDIER'S REFUGE
The Tuttle Sisters of Coho Cove • by Sabrina York
Football star Jax Stringfellow was the bane of Natalie Tuttle's high school existence. A traumatic military tour transformed her former crush from an arrogant, mean-spirited jock into a father figure for her nephews. But can the jaded TV producer trust her newfound connection with this kinder, gentler, *sexier* Jax?

#2987 THEIR ALL-STAR SUMMER
Sisters of Christmas Bay • by Kaylie Newell
Marley Carmichael is back in Christmas Bay, ready to make her baseball-announcing dreams come true. When a one-night stand with sexy minor-league star Owen Taylor ends with a surprise pregnancy, life *and* love throw her the biggest curveball yet!

#2988 A TASTE OF HOME
Sisterhood of Chocolate & Wine • by Anna James
Layla Williams is a spoiled princess—or so Wall Streeter turned EMT Shane Kavanaugh thought. But the captivating chef is so much more than he remembers. When her celebrated French restaurant is threatened by a hostile investor, he'll use all his business—and romance—skills to be the hometown hero Layla needs!

HARLEQUIN
PLUS

Try the best multimedia subscription service for romance readers like you!

Read, Watch and Play.

Experience the easiest way to get the romance content you crave.

Start your **FREE TRIAL** at
<u>www.harlequinplus.com/freetrial</u>.